Jordan Valley Miss

Susan Spess

Jordan Valley Miss
COPYRIGHT 2020 by Susan Spess Shay

All scripture quotations, unless otherwise indicated, are taken from the Holy Bible, New International Version(R), NIV(R), Copyright 1973, 1978, 1984, 2011 by Biblica, Inc.™ Used by permission of Zondervan. All rights reserved worldwide. www.zondervan.com
Scripture quotations, marked KJV are taken from the King James translation, public domain. Scripture quotations marked DR, are taken from the Douay Rheims translation, public domain.
Scripture texts marked NAB are taken from the *New American Bible, revised edition* Copyright 2010, 1991, 1986, 1970 Confraternity of Christian Doctrine, Washington, D.C. and are used by permission of the copyright owner. All Rights Reserved. No part of the New American Bible may be reproduced in any form without permission in writing from the copyright owner.

Cover Art by *Nicola Martinez*
White Rose Publishing, a division of Pelican Ventures, LLC
www.pelicanbookgroup.com PO Box 1738 *Aztec, NM * 87410

Publishing History
First White Rose Edition, 2020
Electronic Edition ISBN 978-1-5223-0334-3
Paperback Edition ISBN 9781522303671
Published in the United States of America

Dedication

To all the ministers and their wives who've been a part of my Christian walk--from Roy Blizzard, Ronnie Epps, Tom Moll, through Rusty Westerfield, Bruce DeLay, and Joe Ray Reeves, and now David Logsdon, our current pastor at FC3.
Thank you! I love you all.

1

The lights blinked out, flashed on, and then went out again.

Really? A little snow and ice, and bam! No electricity? Eli Daniels clenched his jaw to muffle the exasperation before it could escape. *What am I doing in Jordan Valley, Oklahoma?* As if he didn't know the answer to that one. "You OK, Brandi baby?"

His four-year-old daughter stared at him wide-eyed from her spot near, but not *too* near, the blazing fireplace. Her little mouth turned down.

He gave her what he hoped was a confident smile. "The storm knocked out the electricity. It's OK."

She stared at him for another moment before going back to playing with her dolls in the only bright spot in the room. He probably should sit on the floor and play with her—he'd learned how to in the last six months—but he had to finish his sermon. With only four days left to get it ready, he'd already put it off for too long.

Eli made his way through the dimness to his study. Without firelight, the room was shadowed in semi-darkness. He opened the second drawer on the right side of his desk to get the LED headband he knew would be there. He hadn't been able to control other things in his life—well, people—but he could control objects, and depend on them to be where he put them. He checked to see if the batteries still worked, put on headband, and made his way back to the living room.

Brandi didn't seem to realize he'd left the room.

He picked his way past her to his chair and opened his Bible. "What does the LORD require of you? To ac—" The intense light from the headband washed Micah's words right off the page. Eli adjusted the beam, so the brilliance was off center of the Scripture. "Act justly and to love mercy and to walk humbly with yo—" Frustration burned in Eli's chest. He slammed the Bible closed with a smack.

He glanced at his daughter, and his stomach clenched. He probably didn't need the child guard gate to keep her from getting near the raised hearth, but it helped his peace of mind. "Why did you take your dolls' clothes off, Brandi?" he asked. He put a little tease in his voice and hoped for a smile from her.

His four-year-old daughter blinked in the brightness of the headlamp aimed her direction. His wife had told him when they'd bought Brandi her first doll, *That's what little girls do.* His gut tightened as he remembered that happy day. It seemed like yesterday, a thousand painful years ago. And he still didn't understand naked dolls or much about females.

Brandi glanced at him, her big eyes sad, just as they'd been for the past half-year, and shrugged.

Come on, Brandi. Talk to me. "What's that doll's name?"

Another shrug.

Maybe later. Next week. Or next month. "Want to watch it snow? We might be able to go sledding tomorrow if it's not too cold." *And if I can find a hill that low, and slow, and safe enough.*

Her face brightened and, abandoning her still naked dolls, she hopped up, ran to him and jumped into his lap.

He carried her to the window that looked out onto the side yard and pushed back the curtains. The huge flakes were much bigger than the snow that had fallen when they'd lived in Dallas. Of course, Jordan Valley, Oklahoma, was several hundred miles north of Dallas, but a long way south of Kansas City, where he'd grown up.

They call this part of Oklahoma Green Country? Nothing green about it today. He pointed to the place where a bush grew in the V of the porch and steps. "See that white hump right there? That's the bush that scratched you yesterday."

She nodded, but of course, didn't answer.

When would she answer? *When she's ready,* more than one doctor had told him. *Be patient.* But patience wasn't something they taught at the seminary. At least, he hadn't learned it. What the doc hadn't said was, *It's your fault she's not talking.* But Eli knew it was his fault.

Eli started to shift Brandi so she could see the other direction, but she held tight to his neck. "What's wrong?" He followed her gaze. Snow was falling so hard and fast that looking out was like trying to see through Grandmother's heavy lace curtains. "What in the world?" Bright colors peeked through the flurry. *Children? Out in some of the worst weather in Oklahoma history?*

Frowning, he set Brandi on the floor, went to the door, and stepped onto the porch to squint through the storm. There was at least one adult, carrying a child and dragging more up the slight incline between the parsonage and the daycare next door. He dashed onto the steps.

The cold bit hard, causing his entire body to clench. Sleet mixed with the snow, the wind driving it like needles into his exposed skin. Why hadn't he grabbed his coat like most sane people would have? Too late now. He needed to help the woman and kids before frostbite set in for them or him. Back in KC, he'd seen that happen more than once, and the result wasn't pretty.

"Shut the door, Brandi, and keep out the cold. I'll be right back!"

Eli struggled up the slight rise as the snow grew deeper. He gave himself a mental forehead smack as he slid, caught himself, and jump-stepped across his yard into the open space between their house and the daycare.

All he could hear was the faint click of falling flakes as they accumulated on the ground. He hurried faster as the woman and children worked to stay on their feet. As he reached the group, he could see that the last person was also an adult, wearing what looked like camo coveralls. Concern reverberated through him. He took the little girl the first woman had on her hip, startling both of them as he lifted the girl from her arms. "Taking a stroll?"

—"Wha—" Her gaze met his from between her knitted cap and the scarf, wrapped so high on her face it covered her nose. Her eyes were a dark hazel. Recognition flared. "No ellllec—"

"How about we talk about it inside? Come on." Eli took the next child, who looked exhausted, and put her on his shoulders, then grabbed the woman's snow-encrusted mitten. He waited until they'd all held hands again and then took off for the house. He kept his gaze on the porch to be sure Brandi didn't come out.

The group slowed him—short people, short legs, short steps. The other kid was a little boy, whose legs weren't long enough to clear the snow. Eli stopped and dragged the boy to him. "If I put you on my back, can you hang on?"

The boy nodded hard, relief in his eyes.

Eli lifted him. The kid found a place to hold on and clung like a tick on a dog. The kids' combined weight was probably at least a hundred pounds. In his powerlifting days, one hundred pounds of dead weight had been one of his goals. But this was different. Because the weights had been a lump of steel or because now he was too numb to feel it? Or maybe it was the adrenalin caused by the fear for all of them.

After what seemed like eternity, but couldn't have been more than several long, freezing minutes, with his leg muscles burning while the rest of him felt as if he were covered with a layer of ice, he finally got them to the house. He let the girl slide from his hip, swung the boy off his back and finally lifted the girl from his shoulders.

The woman in camo herded them onto the porch where they kicked off boots.

He turned to the woman he'd towed for forty or so yards. "Can you climb those stairs?" he yelled over the wind.

She nodded and shuffled to the first step, where she tripped. Eli grabbed the back of her coat and pulled her upright. She stood for a minute as if unable to remember how her legs worked. Bending his rapidly freezing knees, he grabbed her around her waist and lifted her. Three steps later, they were on the porch. He walked to the door before setting her down.

Once in the house, the woman in camo dropped her coveralls and helped the children out of their snowsuits. "Come on, kids. Let's warm up by the fire."

The first woman had defrosted enough to shake her head. "Nice, Star. Just throw all the snowsuits and jackets on the floor."

"The kids were freezing, Glory," Camo woman snapped. "Besides, Brandi needed some company, didn't you, Brandi?"

"And *your* big sister just loves to pick up after you," the first woman answered. Bending stiffly, she gathered their things. "All right if I take these to the mudroom?" she asked through chattering teeth. Unlike the others, she didn't have a snowsuit—just a jacket.

"Sure. It's where I'm heading, too. Do you think they'll get the electricity back on soon?"

"Depends on what's wrong, but I doubt it." In the

dim light, her eyes looked huge. "The kids' mom is stuck in the city. The expressway is closed, so she can't get home. The power is out, we don't have any way to keep warm next door, and since this is *our* church's parsonage," — her eyes twinkled as if she were teasing just a little—"we belong here. You might be stuck with us for several days."

Kids for Brandi to play with as she did before? Kids she might have so much fun with that she'll forget to be silent and say something?

"Well, in that case, welcome."

"Thank you."

They stopped in the door of the mudroom, where he'd just finished installing a row of hooks on one side and a row of shelves on the other.

She stared. "Been doing a little work in here, have we?"

"Yeah. Now the mudroom is actually useable." Eli thought about the hours it had taken him to install the "easy to use" shelving and was tired all over again. He tugged off his now wet shirt. When the fabric cleared his face, he saw her frown again, but this time she aimed her glare at him. Probably the tattoo encircling his biceps. Couldn't be his muscle tone. *Me, vain? Meh, could be.* "They're tribal bands," he told her as if she'd asked.

She just nodded while she took off her mittens and tried to unzip her coat.

"I got them years ago before I met God."

She fiddled ineffectively with her zipper. With only knit gloves on, she probably had numb fingers.

"Want some help?" At her nod, he reached up and took hold of the zipper with one hand and the surrounding fabric with the other. The metal teeth were stuck or, more likely, frozen. A drip of icy water caught him on the back of the neck as he forced the zipper. Thank goodness, he was still tingly numb, so it didn't matter. Finally, he worked it free. As the zipper moved down, his hand bumped into something hard, stopping him. Couldn't be her body, no one froze that hard and lived to tell about it. His mind raced. Pacemaker? Old fashioned hearing aid? Concealed weapon? "What's that?"

She frowned slightly, as if surprised by his question. "It's my camera."

"You brought a camera? Why?"

She shrugged.

For some reason, that shrug tickled him. "Because of the dangerously low temperatures, you dragged three kids through a blizzard in the hope that I'd be home, and you remembered to grab your camera?" He tried to conceal his grin. "What if we hadn't been here?"

"I saw smoke coming from your chimney, so I knew someone had to be here, and besides"—she dug in her pocket—"I have a key."

That hit him in the gut. With a key, anyone could walk into his house anytime they wanted and do anything they wanted, and he couldn't control a thing. They could even kidnap the only person he cared about in this world. Maybe, hopefully, he'd misunderstood. "Did you say you have a key to my house?"

"I have a key to my neighbor's house *and* my church's parsonage." She lifted her chin. "And if you hadn't been here, I'd have come in and built a fire myself."

Fear bit deep at the idea of anyone having access to his house. "Who all has keys to the parsonage?"

"Only us. Since we're next door, it only makes sense—"

He snatched the key from between her fingers.

Reaching out, she gently covered his fingers with her small, frigid hands and took back the key. "You have a key to our place, too, in your cupboard. It's just in case we ever lock ourselves out. Neighbors do that for each other here."

Small towns. He'd let her keep the key. If they used it without his permission, he'd forget about asking the church board and what neighbors do for each other, and change all the locks. "Better get that scarf and hat off, or you'll get colder and wetter."

She dragged off the dripping wraps.

"I've met you before, haven't I?"

"I'm Glory Matthews. I played the piano at church on Sunday," she answered, raising an eyebrow. "And I was on the pulpit committee that hired you."

"You're one up on most of the membership, then. You've heard two of my sermons now."

Apparently she didn't get his lame joke, because she stared at him, her mouth flat.

He changed the subject. "Is that your sister in there with the kids?"

"Yes. That's Star."

Glory and Star. He hid another smile. Names like that, he'd remember. "Glory and Star. Nice names. Do you have any other siblings?"

"A brother named Cutter." She shivered.

Which reminded Eli how wet her clothes were. "I'll be right back. Do any of the others need dry clothes?"

"No. The kids all had snowsuits and Star had coveralls, so they should be all right."

He took the stairs two at a time. In his bedroom, he found a pair of sweats that had shrunk over the years and dropped them down the staircase to her along with a towel.

Back in his room, he untied his slush-covered shoestrings, shoved his joggers from his feet and stripped off the soggy jeans. He padded to the bathroom, draped them over the tub and grabbed another towel. After a brisk rub, he put on a faded gray sweatsuit. He kept forgetting there was no electricity. Each time he entered a room, he flicked on the light switch, then immediately turned it off again.

When he went back downstairs, Brandi and the other girls were playing with her naked dolls.

Star was doing something with a circle of string and the little boy.

Glory wore his faded-out sweats, and even though they'd shrunk, they were so big, the top kept slipping off her shoulder.

She gave him a thankful grin from where she knelt near the fire. Her face, which had seemed kind of ordinary, look beautiful with that smile.

Focus on the children. Make them feel at home. But how? He'd been in a church where he had a youth minister and an army of volunteers to deal with the children. He really didn't know how to relate to any kids except Brandi. He thought back to the preacher he'd had when he was growing up. The man had been their only minister—no youth pastors, no associates— and Eli had loved him. The man who had introduced him to God and made him want to go into the ministry. Maybe Eli should give him a call so he could help him remember…

Maybe Eli could try to act like his mentor while dealing with other peoples' children. "You haven't introduced me to these fine-looking kids yet, Miss Glory and Miss Star."

"These are the Emorys," Star answered as she held the string for the boy to stick his hand through. "This is Liam tangled in my string." She leaned toward the child and laughed as if she'd taken lessons from a wicked witch.

"And the girls are Sophie and Zoey." Glory went on as if she and Star were a verbal a tag team. "Sophie's oldest, then Liam, and Zoey is the baby."

"I am not a baby," the little girl replied, arms folded, her pointy chin in the air. "I'm a big girl."

"Yes, you are. A big, three-year-old girl." Glory pulled the girl to her. "When I said you were the baby, I meant you were the last one born. The baby of your family, like Star's the baby of our family."

"Oh." Zoey's eyes grew round with wonder. "Miss

Star is the baby, too?"

"I am not a baby," Star teased.

The kids laughed, and his heart pounded. Could one of the chuckles be Brandi's?

"I'm really glad you have a fireplace here and not just a woodstove. We can cook dinner over the fire if you have wienies and we can find sticks."

His laughter surprised him, he'd not laughed in ages. "I have wienies, but I'm afraid our sticks were buried under all that ice."

She frowned and looked at her sister, who shrugged and went back to her game. He could almost see Glory's mind working as she tried to think of a way to prepare them.

"But the kitchen has a gas stove, so we won't starve," he said to save her the trouble.

Her smile was broad, and just a little crooked. "Good. I wish we had one next door."

"You really don't have a way to warm the daycare when the electricity is off?"

Glory shook her head. "No open flames at all. Our place is all electric—"

"Thanks to Mom." Star interrupted.

"*And* the electric co-op," Glory said. "Mom is very safety-conscious, so when she built the daycare on the front of the house, she made us all electric." She shook her head as she rolled her eyes. "*All*."

"Your parents are still living?"

"Well, our mother is." Glory shrugged, her gaze shifting slightly from his face. "We haven't seen or heard from our father since the day he left when I was nearly three."

Ouch. That sounded painful. He changed the subject slightly. "Where's your mother?"

"On a cruise"—she made quotation marks with her fingers—"with Aunt Rosemary. They have a sixth sense about the best time to be gone."

"Why did you say it like that?" He lowered his voice. "Aren't they really on a cruise?"

Glory shrugged, her shoulder slipping out of the sweatshirt again. She pulled the cloth back into place. "Oh, I don't know where they are. They might be on a cruise, but what they're doing is working on another children's book. When they get back, they'll help out in the daycare long enough to test the book on the kids."

Curiosity got to him. "And the book?"

"After they test it on the daycare kids, they'll tweak it and send it to their publisher. In a few months, we'll have a new Sistery Mystery on the shelf."

"Sistery Mysteries, by Beany and Sam?" He'd heard of the books since becoming a single parent, but Brandi was a little young for them yet. Miranda had wanted to write children's books, too. Back in the day, she'd told Brandi lots of stories. He swallowed past the thickening in his throat brought on by reminders of how he'd failed Miranda. And how his brother, Jeremiah, hadn't. Clenching his jaw, he forced the thought away. *Not now.*

"Beany and Sam is their pen name. The books are really by Ginger and Rosemary Matthews."

"I'll have to read them one of these days."

"Brandi will probably like them." She glanced

over her shoulder at the kids playing near the fire. "Got enough to feed this whole gang?"

"Yeah. We—I—learned the first year out of seminary to always to have plenty of something on hand. We can have wienies or spaghetti. Your choice." He listened to the little girls' giggles, his heart beating faster. *Please God, was one Brandi?*

When dinner was ready, they spread a plastic tablecloth on the floor in front of the fireplace and told the kids they were having a picnic.

Brandi loved it. Eli could tell because the sadness left her eyes and they sparkled, almost as if she might laugh. But of course, she didn't.

After dinner, the other children looked a little droopy. He grabbed pillows and quilts for everyone from the linen closet, which the church had stocked well. When all the kids had a place to sleep, he took down the antique popcorn popper. He threw in a handful of kernels, grasped the long handle and held it over the hot coals in the fireplace. Shaking it, he waited for the corn to pop.

Eli scrambled to think of ways to keep the kids from missing their mom or worse, start crying. His mind crept back to Miranda and her storytelling. "Do you know about the little boy who saved a nation?" he asked, trying to keep his voice light. "His name was David. His big brothers were in the army fighting another nation, called the Philistines. Now the 'Stines had a great warrior, a giant of a man, named Goliath!"

By the time the kids had finished the popcorn, and he'd finished the story, they were snuggled down on their pallets, too sleepy to be homesick. Soon, they dropped off.

He thought he heard the click of a camera as he went out to the service porch, but he didn't see a flash. He carried in a big armload of wood, stacked it where he could easily reach it, and sat on the floor between Brandi and the fireplace so he could feed the fire through the night. Before he lay down to sleep, he glanced around the room one last time and mentally ticked off responsibilities, looking for anything he'd failed to do. Kids warm, dry, and fed. Everyone with a place to sleep. Windows locked, doors locked, everyone happy, filled, and satisfied. *What else? Am I forgetting anything?*

The room looked golden because of the flames. The furniture, floor, kids, Star in his recliner and Glory, lying on the sofa, all looked as if they had been coated with gilt. The fire glinted in Glory's eyes, giving him the strangest feeling she was watching him.

~*~

Glory came aware slowly, keeping her eyes tightly shut. If she opened them, she'd never get back to sleep. As she lay there, her insides buzzed as if she'd swallowed a blowfly. Wiggling her hips, she tried to get comfortable as she flung out her left arm. It didn't go anywhere. In her bed, she had all kinds of room for sprawling. Where was she? She finally remembered yesterday.

It hadn't just snowed. It had rained, froze, and

sleeted, too. They'd lost power and still had the Emory kids with them. Janyce was stuck in the city. And their new minister had all of them in his house. He wasn't overly thrilled about it, either.

But no one in Jordan Valley had electricity or phone service. People who didn't have cell phones didn't have a way to contact anyone.

On that thought, the blowfly turned into a bumblebee. She had things to do. People to check on. She made her list of things to do in her head.

First: Feed kiddos.

No, wait. Probably ought to get the kids dressed and their borrowed nightwear back to the minister and then feed them. What was there to eat? Maybe she should wake the preacher—she remembered his dark, intense gaze, his gorgeous mouth, and the way his smile slowly bloomed a little at a time as if it were sneaking up on him. The bumblebee inside her exploded into a whole colony.

So much for being a mature thirty-three-year-old woman of the world. Well, she had lived on her own in Oklahoma City for almost a year, so she was at least a woman of the state. *Back to my list.*

One: Get the kids dressed.

Two: Breakfast.

Three: Check on Miss Charlotte and Mrs. Jackson. Two octogenarians discovered as frozen as popsicles in Jordan Valley would probably make national news, and not in a good way. Oh, and Halle. Of course, knowing Halle, she'd worked through the storm and didn't know anything had happened except that she didn't have electricity. But in her normal Halle-esque manner, she'd probably built herself a generator with junk from one of the auctions she frequented, and then worked through the storm.

Glory decided to check on her anyway. First, though, she needed to get up. She felt for the blanket covering her and remembered the quilt. Last night, Eli had handed her a hand-made quilt in shades of blue and yellow and white that was so perfectly beautiful, she'd wanted to frame it. The pattern was a Lone Star. Not an easy one to piece, yet the center of the star had been precise, and the hand quilting was tiny, even stitches. It was so soft, when she wrapped up in it, she'd felt swaddled in down. And hers wasn't the only quilt he'd handed out as casually as if they were army blankets. Everyone got one. She'd seen a Dresden Plate, and a Log Cabin. Star covered up with a Road to Oklahoma made in faded red, white and blue. The man had a real treasure trove and acted as if he didn't know it.

Men. Maybe she could get pictures of them before she left. Glory hated to, but she needed to leave her quilt behind and find her clothes. Would they be dry after hanging in the frigid mudroom all night? Freeze-dried, maybe? Sitting up, she decided to take the quilt with her. The warmth from the fireplace only went so far. She found her camera and slung it around her neck, slid her feet into slippers Eli had loaned her, about ten sizes too big, and scuffed to the mudroom. On her way past a window, she glanced out at the daycare. The ice made the weird shape of their old farmhouse—which had sprouted a daycare on front when she was almost too small to remember—kind of pretty. She focused through the eyepiece of her camera and snapped the shutter. In the mudroom, she found her clothes still wet and very, very cold. *Looks like I'll be hanging around in the preacher's sweats for a while longer.*

By the time she shuffled back to the narrow kitchen, the aromatic warmth of coffee brewing drew her to the country kitchen like a magnet. She pulled the quilt around her more tightly and followed the fragrance. "Uum. Brother Eli, your coffee smells wonderful."

He glanced sharply at her, his look nearly stabbing her. "Don't call me that."

The roughness of his voice surprised her. "Don't call you what?"

"Just call me Eli," His voice sounded gravelly.

A lot of people in their church called their ministers brother. If Eli snapped at them as he just did her, he wouldn't be very popular. But then, it could just be normal morning grouchiness. Her brother, Cutter, had always been grumpy in the mornings, and they'd learned to ignore him. But who wanted a minister they had to ignore? She slid past him to find mugs. She pulled out three, set them near the stove, and then found creamer and sugar. As she turned around, his fixed gaze stopped her. Leaning against the tiled counter as she moved around his kitchen, his desperado good looks robbed what she'd been doing right out of her mind. "I...uh...I've been in this kitchen many times before you...uh...moved in." She lifted her right eyebrow, sending him a questioning glance.

"I see." His eyes lit up before his mouth caught the grin, and though he seemed to fight it, his lips curved and spread in a devastating smile. Her bumblebees made a return.

Grabbing a honey-colored chair, she quickly sat before her knees gave way. His focus made her feel as if he could see through her, know her thoughts, her feelings, everything. Her entire face stung with heat.

He turned back to the cupboard. "Hope everyone likes cereal."

"I'm sure it'll be fine."

He shot her a straight look as if he hadn't heard her.

She nodded hard.

He pulled out disposable bowls and eating utensils, piled them on the counter, and then got out cereal. Full-sized boxes of what seemed to be every kind of cereal known to kid-dom.

She lined up the boxes, snugging them close to create more room on the small table made for two. "Remember when we were kids and used to have a variety pack of cereal? Small boxes, assorted kinds. My mom always bought those because we changed our mind about what we wanted to eat a lot."

He growled as he tried to fit in the last box, or maybe he grumbled something under his breath. It was hard to tell. With a sigh, he finally laid the box on top of the others and shook his head. "Brandi has a brilliant future in product testing. She's an advertiser's dream."

And you can't say no. Glory focused on the boxes of cereal. "You can't even donate them to a food pantry once they're open."

He chuckled. "She's tried every one, but most have had very little taken out. She almost always goes back to Sergeant Sugar or Sweetie Bear Cereal."

"But at least she'll try something new. That's a good thing. Some people can't even change their hairstyle." She might not have much she was good at—not like Star and her baking or Mom with the children's books—but at least she was good at building up kids.

With a quirk of an eyebrow, Eli's gaze wandered toward the front room.

Glory guessed at his thoughts—her sister and her hair the color of crude oil. "Star, on the other hand, changes her hair color about as often as the wind blows. And sometimes with blinding success."

His soft chuckle sent heat swirling in her gut. What was wrong with her?

"Do all of you—Star and your mom and her sister—live next door together?"

"No. Star has an apartment downtown. I live next door with our brother. Mom and Rosemary stay at the house some, but Rosemary has a place in the city where they spend time, too."

"You have a brother?"

She cleared the thickness from her throat. "Yeah, his name's Cutter. Remember, I told you? He's run away from home for the first time in his life, but he'll be home by farm time.

"You have a farm?"

"Hundred and sixty acres." Glory nodded. "The daycare is part of the farm. The family's owned it since our great-great grandma made the land run. Originally, Jordan Valley stopped at the post office, but the town kind of grew over to us."

"Where's your brother now?"

"He's in New Orleans, on vacation. Good thing, too. We might not have had enough cereal to go around."

He shook his head, his wry smile making it hard for her to breathe. "I could always do a grocery store run."

"If there's one open." She sidled past him to the fridge and opened the door. "Is it OK if I give the kids some of this orange juice? I'll buy you a new jug when things clear up."

"Sure. No prob—" He stopped mid-word, concern creasing his face. "I smell smoke, and I shouldn't. That chimney draws really well. Do you think a burning ember fell on the floor?"

She would have told him the fire was dying, the lack of heat causing the smoke to escape out the front of the fireplace rather than up the chimney if he hadn't practically run from the kitchen. It had to be the dwindling flame putting odor in the air, because it would be unlikely for an ember to escape his safeguards.

After finding paper cups in the pantry, she poured four servings of orange juice and then followed him to the living room. His muscles flexed beneath his sweatsuit as he tossed wood on the fire. She couldn't help but admire the view. She swallowed hard. "Anybody hungry?"

Liam popped up, of course. He was always hungry these days. The girls were a little slower in waking.

Star ended a call on her cell phone. "Better eat, guys. Your mom is heading this way to get you."

When Eli had replaced the fireplace screen, they spread the plastic tablecloth on the floor.

The girls all wanted cereal with a princess on the box. Liam had Sweetie Bear. Star, who lived by the motto, *I'm number three so I try hardest,* chose a super healthy cereal that Eli must have picked up by mistake. Her bowl looked as if it were filled with dried stems and seeds.

Glory followed Liam's example and ate the sugary sweet cereal she'd loved since she was a kid.

Eli did, too.

Glory drained her coffee. "When does Janyce think she'll get here?"

Star glanced at her phone. "Depending on how well they cleared the roads, she should be here in a few minutes."

"I've been thinking, someone needs to check on Miss Charlotte and Mrs. Jackson." Glory smiled at Eli. "That is, if I can borrow these sweats."

He lifted one eyebrow. "I wouldn't want you going without them."

Embarrassment flashed through her, quickly chased by a tingling sensation all the way to her toes.

This preacher was like none she'd ever met. She swallowed hard and tried to hold back the burn spreading across her shoulders to her neck.

2

"Pull into Sparkle." Glory commanded. "Right there!" She pointed.

Steering carefully, Eli followed Glory's instructions. For someone who'd wanted to walk, she sure didn't mind telling him how to drive. He rolled his eyes but kept his mouth shut. He glanced down the state highway that doubled as Jordan Valley's main road. Clear. Well, not Main Street itself. It was still snow and ice covered with only a little sand to help with traction, but at least there was no traffic. In fact, they could shoot a cannon down the street and never hit a thing, if someone had a cannon.

Why was he making this call on a pair of old ladies, anyway? His stomach tensed, giving him an all-over uneasiness. This was a job for the assistant minister if he had one. He'd never done this kind of thing, except with close friends or board members. Going into strange homes just wasn't his thing. He should have explained that to Glory. His gift, if one could call it that, was speaking and dealing with the congregation as a whole—from a safe distance.

Besides, the roads were awful. This part of Oklahoma seemed almost as bad as Dallas. *When snow hits, the world stops.* Except, it seemed, for Sparkle. Whatever that was.

He slowly made what must be an illegal turn and bumped to a stop in front of the shop. "What is this place?"

Glory unbuckled her seatbelt and picked up her ever-present camera from the seat beside her. "It's Halle's shop. You probably met her Sunday. Anyway, she has a coffee shop and sells gifts, antiques, flowers, all kinds of stuff."

So why were they there? "And you need to check on her?"

"Not really. I want to see if she has soup ready. We'll take some to Miss Charlotte and Mrs. Jackson." She was out of the car almost before she finished talking.

He followed her into the store, and as he entered, a delicious aroma made his mouth water. The fragrance was like fresh baked fruitcake—he sniffed again—with the underlying odor of . . . sawdust?

The store reminded him of his childhood. Antique furniture gave him a cozy feeling as if his grandparents were alive and living here. An old wardrobe like the one they'd had stood open with a throw hanging inside. A treadle sewing machine, standing near it, had a delicate china tea set on top. And some farm wife's well-used and loved farm table was covered with candles. A trunk with a key in the lock stood open to display handmade knitted items. Old suitcases stacked in graduating sizes served as an end table next to a vintage rocking chair.

But the fruity aroma kept pulling him toward the next room. He stepped through the arching door into a space with tables scattered all around. Some old, some just odd. One had gargoyles carved into the legs. Another was a well-used white metal ice cream table like the ones he'd seen in period movies. Still others were old folding card tables his mother had played Bridge on back in the day.

Glory moved toward him with two quart-sized containers. The cereal he'd eaten earlier was quickly leaving his memory, while the heady scent nearly made him dizzy. "I hope one of those is for me," he said.

"Nope." She held the containers away from him as if he might wrestle them from her. "We'll come back and get some for us later. These are for the sisters."

"Hey, Preach! Good morning!" a lilting voice called.

He turned to wave at the blonde holding a cookie sheet pan. The woman stood in the kitchen area that was sectioned off only by a long counter.

"That's Halle," Glory murmured, a teasing gleam in her eye. "Remember her now?"

He shook his head. "Good morning."

"Y'all be careful out on those slick streets, now. Jordan Valley doesn't have much of a snow removal department." With another wave, she turned to set what must have been some kind of fruitcake cookies in the oven.

He walked with Glory back through the antiques when the words the woman had spoken registered.

Had she called him Preach? As in Preacher? <u>Him</u>? Since when was he just a preacher? He was an evangelist. Class Orator, voted by the students and professors at his seminary—His irritation sputtered out. He might have been at the top when he graduated, but no more. That was the reason he'd left his mega-church in Dallas and ended up in tiny Jordan Valley making home calls on old ladies. He wasn't worthy of a church like that. Maybe he was just a preacher who deserved to be called Preach.

Memories of his triumphs and victories, which he'd concentrated on time after time when he'd lost everything—which had always lifted him when his failures had started to become obvious—escaped him like air from a popped balloon.

He took the soup from Glory and followed her out to the car like a well-trained collie. When she was inside and buckled, he handed the stew back to her. Rounding the car, he slipped on the ice and nearly fell. What kind of town didn't even sand the sidewalks, much less clear them?

The kind that would accept you for a minister.

Righting himself, he made it to the car. He followed Glory's directions to Miss Charlotte's house. The driveway was empty, so if she had a car, it was tucked away in the tiny garage, and neither the sidewalk nor the driveway was clear.

Good thing he'd remembered to toss the snow shovel into the back of his SUV before they left the house. He thought he was doing it in case they got stuck somewhere.

Apparently, Someone had other ideas.

He left the engine running, but before he could open his door, Glory was out of hers, carrying one of the containers of soup. Unwilling to let her try to navigate alone, he stepped out and took her arm above the elbow.

She glanced up at him with a half-smile. "Hey, I saw you slip on the ice downtown. If you go down here, don't take me with you."

He held her dark hazel gaze and tried to hide the smile pulling at him. "I might need you to catch me. You don't want to hunt for another minister this soon, do you?"

Her laughter warmed him, even with wind swirling snow between the houses. They walked up the steps to a square box of a house, covered in old fashioned, rusty-pink colored shingles and knocked on a screen door. Several moments passed before an older woman with a round face filled with soft, sweet wrinkles opened it. Eli remembered her. She'd played the organ so loud on Sunday he hadn't been able to hear the piano at all.

"Oh, Glory and the preacher! Come in. Come in!" She unlatched the screen and pushed it open. She was wearing her coat and a pair of mittens. Inside the house was nearly as frigid as outside, but as cold as it was, the smile never left her face. "I'd offer you some coffee, but I've lost my electric."

"Everyone else in town has, too." Glory glanced at him. Alarm widened her eyes, and rather than hand the woman the soup, she tucked it under her arm.

"We've come to get you."

Miss Charlotte's mouth dropped open as she shook her head. "Oh, no. I'm fine."

But Eli thought he saw relief on her face.

"You might be fine, but your sister needs you." Glory sounded firm. "All she has is that fireplace to keep her warm, and she could use some help feeding it. So get what you need together. We're going."

"Oh. I didn't realize." Miss Charlotte practically trotted off.

While she was gone, Eli turned to Glory. "Give me the soup. I'll put it back in the car with the other batch. I'll shovel the steps and sidewalk before we take her out there." He reached for the soup, but Glory held onto it for a moment. He glanced down to find a smile in her eyes.

"I was hoping you would." Her voice was low.

Something sparked inside him, causing his heart to charge and beat a little faster. He'd known that feeling before, but it had died. And it had been so long since he'd felt it, he'd nearly forgotten what it was. Or maybe it was all in his head.

He took the soup to the car and put it near the other container under the heater vent, then got his shovel from the cargo area. The snow moved easily, but the ice beneath it took a little more work. By the time he finished, he'd unzipped his jacket and was thinking about losing it altogether. With a small path cleared, he knocked on the door. "Ready, ladies?"

Miss Charlotte stepped onto the porch and looked around. After a moment, she hugged him. "Oh, you sweet boy. I'm ashamed to leave now after you've done all this work."

"That work will still be here when you get back. Come on. We need to take you to your sister's house." *Wherever that is.*

To get the older woman out of the cold and off the ice as quickly as possible, he helped her into the nearest seat, the one right behind his, while Glory got in the front. Stowing the shovel, he got into the driver's seat.

Glory had turned the heat on high.

With me sweating like this? He reached to turn it down.

Glory caught his hand. "Miss Charlotte is still shivering," she whispered.

"OK," he answered, adjusting the vents, so they pointed toward the back. He put the truck in reverse and backed cautiously into the street.

Glory directed him to the other side of Main Street and a two-story white house, just about four blocks away. A red brick chimney rose out of the snow and ice, dividing the house in half, but no smoke came from it.

"No smoke. Something's wrong." Her words were barely a whisper.

He thought about the name, Jackson, but couldn't bring a face to mind. No surprise. Afraid of what they'd find, he kept his voice as low. "Stay in the car." He opened his door, stepped out, and then stuck his head back inside and glanced at Miss Charlotte. "I'll make these sidewalks safer to walk on." He went to the back of the car to get the shovel and saw a full rick of wood on a stand at the side of the house. Since it was situated on the south, it was fairly protected. So why wasn't anything coming from that chimney? Extremely worried now, he went to the door and knocked.

The quilt-wrapped woman who answered the door might have looked like a cord-thin version of Miss Charlotte, but the lines in her face made him doubt she'd have the same sweet disposition. Then she opened her mouth and proved it. "Are we paying you so little to preach, you have to make extra by shoveling sidewalks?"

She'd complained about his "garish" tie at church. "No, Mrs. Jackson, that's not the problem." He decided to be just as plain spoken. "Glory and I brought your sister to stay with you during this cold spell. I thought it best to clear the sidewalk for her."

"You think it's warmer on this side of town?" Her voice grew harder if that was possible.

"No. But without electricity, she's having a hard time of it."

"As you can see, I don't have electricity, either."

Time for the stern voice he usually reserved for Brandi. He put a little power behind it. "But you do have a fireplace. And I'll carry in enough wood to keep you two warm until spring."

"Wood is expensive these days, young man! And it draws termites."

"I'll buy you a rick to replace it." He thought about ignoring the termite comment but decided against it. "And if it draws termites, you can burn them up." Without waiting for her consent, he turned and started digging through the snow and ice, his irritation fueling him. In record time, he had a path on the sidewalk, the long porch, and the steps cleared. When he got to the car, he opened Miss Charlotte's door and helped her out.

Glory was beside them in seconds, lending a hand.

Miss Charlotte stared at the full rick of wood. "Sister must have been afraid to venture out on the ice to get wood for her fireplace."

Guilt settled in his gut as he thought about the old woman's fear. Falling on the ice for a woman her age would almost certainly mean a broken bone, possibly a hip. Why hadn't he realized her fear instead of arguing with her?

Mrs. Jackson must have heard the car door slam because she stuck her head outside the house. "Well, you've got nothing but a goat path cleared there, Preacher. Sister, be careful you don't fall. I'd have to nurse you if you got a broken hip because there's no one else to do it!"

Glory sighed.

"Isn't he the sweetest thing, Sister?" Miss Charlotte's voice was the exact opposite of Mrs. Jackson's. "He cleared my walks, too. Imagine that!"

When Miss Charlotte and Glory were safely inside, he made his way to the wood and loaded his arms. He carried the first load inside, where Glory knelt in front of the fireplace, arranging kindling. While she built the fire, he went back out and moved about half of the rick to the porch, then filled the wood box in the living room.

"I don't know where you think Charlotte's going to sleep. There are only two bedrooms downstairs here, and the back bedroom is so cold, everything probably has a layer of ice." The old woman's face grew as sharp as a fox's. "Unless you can get up and down the stairs, Charlotte. With the fireplace going, the chimney will keep the front upstairs bedroom warm."

"Oh, Sister. Don't worry about making up a bedroom for me. I'll be fine right here on your couch with your lovely quilts."

It was hard to believe they were sisters.

Glory turned in a complete circle. "Did you make all these quilts yourself, Mrs. Jackson?"

Quilts covered every available surface—folded and stacked on a bookshelf like big, soft encyclopedias, lying on the old brown couch where she must have been trying to stay warm, as well as across chairs flanking a small table filled with drawers and even on top of an old upright piano in the adjacent dining room. Quilts, quilts, quilts.

Mrs. Jackson nodded. "Keeps my hands and brain nimble."

"You ought to sell them." Glory moved closer to the bookshelf and held the camera to her face.

"Sell them? Why, girl, I give them away. The parsonage is probably full of them, unless Mark took them to that nursing home with him, and I doubt if he could."

"You made those, too?" Glory rubbed her cheek across a quilt before putting it back on the chair.

"They're wonderful."

"Well, I don't finish them all by myself." How could a woman make a statement like that and sound as if she were accusing someone of stealing the United States Treasury? "I have some help. When I'm ready to quilt, Charlotte here, and some other women, come over and help me. Charlotte's the best, though. She has smaller and more even stitches than anyone."

"I love helping her," Miss Charlotte said. "Besides, it keeps my fingers moving for my organ playing."

Mrs. Jackson's snort told them she didn't think much of organ music, or maybe it was her sister's ability for which she held little regard. There was something to that. "Where's that little one of yours, Brother Daniels?"

He gritted his teeth at the brother remark. "She's at my house along with some children whose mother got caught in the city. Star's watching them and keeping the fireplace stoked."

"What's your daughter's name?" Mrs. Jackson raised her eyebrows, which made her face look oddly blank. For some reason, her expression worried him.

"Brandi."

"That's what I thought you said in church when you introduced her." Her brows dropped lower than ever while her voice grew sharper and louder, if that were possible. "But I couldn't believe a man of the cloth would name his daughter after a thief that only comes to rob and steal."

"I'm not sure what thief you're talking about, Mrs. Jackson." Of course, he knew. He'd heard it before, but he'd hoped this time, in this town, people would be different. He should have known.

Her thin white hair, already standing on end, waved as she wobbled her head. She glared at him. "Alcohol, man. Alcohol! It robs a family of their hard earned money and steals a man's brains. Why would you name your sweet baby girl after alcohol?"

"We didn't. My wife's maiden name was Brandywine, so we named her after her family. We just shortened it to Brandi and left off the wine."

"You know, there's just about every pattern I can think of here, as well as some appliqued ones." Glory changed the subject as she turned, snapping another picture of the quilts piled all over Mrs. Jackson's living room. "Mrs. Jackson, have you ever talked to Halle about selling your quilts at Sparkle?"

"Why would she want to?" The old woman snorted as if to make her point. "Besides, she has enough junk in that store. Last time I went in to get her to fix a picture frame, I nearly got lost in all her foofaraw."

Eli moved back to the door, ready to escape. "We went in this morning to get you some soup, and I thought she had arranged it very well."

"You got soup? Well, where is it? I'm starving." Mrs. Jackson stopped glaring at him and turned back to Glory.

"It's in the car, which we left running so it would stay warm. I'll get it." Eli emphasized his last words, so Glory wouldn't think she could escape and leave him at Mrs. Jackson's mercy. With the narrow path he'd cleared, he easily navigated the walkway to the car and gave serious thought to leaving. But abandoning Glory to Mrs. Jackson wasn't an option since he tried to live by the old wartime adage, *No man left behind.* Or was that one of the president's educational themes? Whichever it was, he couldn't leave Glory there with the grumpy old woman.

Besides, when Glory was around, Eli could feel the sun, even though he couldn't see it. He nearly slipped at the thought. What right did he have to think about any woman after what he'd been and done? None. He'd better stop, or he'd feel the sun, and she'd get nothing but the burn.

He went back inside with both quarts of soup.

"My goodness, that's too much for two old ladies. Do you think we'll be snowed in for the winter?"

OK, enough, Mrs. Jackson. "What you don't eat, you can set outside and let freeze. Then when the roads are clear again, drive down to Sparkle and see if Halle won't give you money back."

"I don't drive, young man. I ride a bicycle to save the environment."

His pointed words had missed their mark. An unwilling smile curved his mouth at the image of the old woman on a bike.

On the way home, Eli looked at Glory. "I think I'd take a beating before I'd go back to that house."

"I know the secret to sweetening up Mrs. Jackson."

He could hear the smile in her voice without looking at her. "Well, tell me quick. If it'll make that old"—he struggled to keep from calling one of his church members an old bat—"*woman* sweet, I'm for it."

"When you go see her, take Brandi with you."

"And let her snipe at Brandi like she did me? I couldn't do that to my daughter." He shot her a glance to see if she was teasing.

She wasn't. "Mrs. Jackson loves children. She was a first grade teacher and lived by the philosophy that if you teach children to enjoy school right at the start, they'll always love it. Parents used to fight to get their children in her class."

"Hard to believe." He tried to imagine the old woman with a smile on her face, children asking to be near her and giving her hugs. Impossible. "What happened to her? Or does she just hate preachers?"

"Oh, no. She liked you."

"She *liked* me?" *I won't call you a liar. Yet.* "What's she like when she doesn't like someone?"

"*Unbearable.*" Her laugh was short and light. "You know, Jordan Valley is the only place she taught her whole career. She was my teacher in first grade, and she taught it like she had several decades earlier when she first started. We sang every morning, 'to get the day going right,' she always said. And I don't remember one child she ever had to discipline."

"I guess I'll have to remember to live by that scripture, 'A little child shall lead them,' and let Brandi go first."

They stopped at Sparkle, and Glory went in for more soup. Rather than go in and get lost in the nostalgia again, he got out his shovel and cleared the sidewalk between the angled parking space and the front of the shop. He doubted anyone would be out on a day like this in a town that didn't do much to clear the streets, but he might save someone coming for soup from a bad fall.

When Glory came out with a huge container of soup and a grocery bag, he opened the car door so she could get inside, stowed the shovel and climbed behind the wheel again. The next breath he took was rich with a wonderful, yeasty fragrance.

He threw the car into reverse and, tires spinning just a little, backed out of the parking space and headed home. He turned off Main Street onto Apache Drive with a minimum of fish-tailing, and could soon see his house. It wasn't anything like the elegant manse the Dallas church had provided for him, but this church wasn't anything like that one either. It was smaller and friendlier. From what he'd seen so far, there was less "high society" here and more spirituality.

It reminded him of his first days at seminary when all he'd wanted was to be able to learn how to share the adventure of Jesus. Back before he found out what a pleasing tongue and quick wit could do for a man's career.

And how a "successful" minister could lose his soul.

~*~

Glory struggled to get out of the car. She hated to have someone opening the door and helping her. As the number one Matthews kid—oldest wasn't a term she used—she'd learned to be the do-it-for-herself type, and to take care of her mom and siblings. Not be taken care of.

But just as before, Eli came close to her, touching her elbow, ready to catch her, and when he touched her even in that one tiny spot, she grew warm all over. At least, it was better than being cold.

The co-op really needed to get their electricity back on. Soon.

"Why don't you let me carry that bread for you?" he murmured in a tone that said, *so I can eat all three loaves before we get to the door.*

"Ha! No way, Preach." She conjured her sweetest smile. "But I'd appreciate it if you'd carry the soup."

"Is that the kids' mom's car parked in the street?" Eli took the soup as he spoke.

Glory nodded. "She and Star are probably chatting. They're good friends."

"Have I met her?"

"I doubt it. She's a Methodist." Glory stepped into knee-deep snow. Too bad Star and the kids hadn't found the shovels and cleared the way. When they got inside, Glory said a quick hello, grabbed the soup from Eli, and hurried on to the kitchen, where she transferred it to a pan. She soon had it warming over a low flame and the loaves of bread in the oven. While she waited, she went back to the living room to see how the kids were doing.

Star had the children in a semi-circle around the fireplace and, not surprisingly, they were smacking their knees rhythmically. *Going on a Bear Hunt* had been Star's favorite quiet game since they were kids. Sometimes Glory suspected Star worked at the daycare just to have an excuse to play it.

A quiet hiccough drew her attention to the couch where Janyce sat, her hands full of tissues and her eyes red and swollen.

Eli stood a few feet away, looking as if he'd rather face a charging rhino than the crying woman. Facing feminine tears was probably a fair part of his job.

Glory ignored him. "Janyce, hello!"

Janyce replied a sobbing, "Hello."

"What's wrong?" Glory asked, dropping to the couch beside her. She knew the woman had problems. In fact, she was drowning in them, but it was nothing new. They'd been keeping her children for her, without charge, for weeks.

"We've lost everything." The woman tried to whisper, but her voice broke, arching into a wail. She pulled her thin sweater closer. "My temp job in Tulsa is over; we're locked out of our house because I couldn't pay the rent, so our clothes and furniture are gone, and it's too cold now to sleep in the car."

Glory glanced at Eli in time to see him fold his arms in front of him while his jaw grew rock hard—sign language for, *Don't offer my house, because the answer's no.*

It's not your house, Glory wanted to argue, but she knew better. The absolute truth was, the parsonage belonged to the minister as if the deed was in his name. Instead of arguing or cajoling, she made a face at him and put an arm around Janyce. "Have you eaten today?"

The slender woman shook her head. "I'm not hungry."

"If you don't eat, you'll get sick, and then who'll take care of the kids?" She stood and looked at the children before tossing a glance back at Janyce. Glory would have to keep her busy until they could figure something. "Why don't you come help me dish up lunch?"

As they walked to the kitchen, Glory checked the woman's clothes—not nearly warm enough. Janyce looked half frozen, even though the house was toasty warm. Star should have given her a quilt to wrap up in.

Glory pulled out the plastic tablecloth and several spoons, which she handed to Janyce. "Make Star and the kids move so you can spread this right in front of the fireplace. Then put spoons around it for all of us. I'll be there in a moment with the soup."

Shoulders hunched, the woman scurried out of the kitchen. In mere seconds, a movement caught Glory's attention. "Stay in there by the fire, Janyce. I'm almost finished here."

"I'm not Janyce." Eli kept his voice low as he moved so close, his shoulder bumped hers.

Warmth flowed through her, but she wasn't sure if it was from the camaraderie of working together or the size of his shoulders.

Taking down a cutting board and finding a serrated knife, he used a kitchen mitt to reach into the oven for a loaf of bread and started slicing it. "You've been keeping her children without charging her, just to help her out, haven't you?" he murmured, his tone light.

"We do that sometimes for people who need a hand. It's our ministry."

He hesitated. Weighing free babysitting to see if it was worthy of being called a ministry? But he didn't argue. "Not many of the people I know, and I've known some very wealthy ones, would do that. Especially if they knew they wouldn't be repaid."

"Then maybe it's time for you to meet some new people." She poured the last bowl of soup, picked up the tray she'd set the bowls on. "Maybe that's why God brought you to Jordan Valley. So you could get to know the right ones."

After flashing a smile, she stepped around him. *Nice, Glory. Now he'll probably toss the whole bunch of us out into the snow.*

~*~

The right people? Eli's stomach churned as he carefully cut the bread in even slices. *I was the Senior Minister at the largest church in Texas. Every right person in Dallas attended my church and was proud of it. Like an idiot, I was, too. After all, the congregation donated enough money to build a spectacular edifice without us having to go into a cent of debt. Their kids all went to private schools and private colleges. My salary rivaled that of the president of most companies. They were proud to have me as their pastor.*

I graduated at the top of my class at seminary, earned every top award the school gave out that year, and I married a beautiful, talented wife. And the moment they learned of trouble in my marriage, without a word of counsel or help, the church fired me. Yes, the memory still stung.

While he'd served as their minister, he'd believed, as surely as he knew his name was Eli Michael Daniels, that God had rewarded him with that church and that membership. God's way of saying, "I'm pleased."

He'd been wrong.

When Glory and the rest of the committee had visited that church on his last Sunday there, she'd seen the over-the-top beauty of the building, the price of the cars in the parking lot, the obvious wealth of the members. Unlike him, the glitter hadn't fooled her.

Sadly, he wanted it all back.

He picked up the platter and carried it into the living room. What he saw stopped him as if he'd walked face-first into a brick wall.

Glory had everyone in the room, all the children, Star and that other woman—Janet? Janna?—holding hands in front of the fire and giving thanks for the snow—*really?*—the soup, the warmth of the fire and, the biggest surprise of all, for him.

That had to be because she really didn't know him.

He carried the bread over.

Glory said, "Amen," and raised her delicate chin.

He handed her the platter.

"Thank you, Eli."

"Yeah! Thank you, *Ewi*," Liam mimicked.

"No, sir!" his mother responded, heat kindling her

words. "Brother Daniels is an adult and a minister. You'll call him Brother Daniels, Brother Eli, Mister Eli or Mister Daniels. Don't ever let me hear you call an adult by their first name. Do you understand me?"

Liam dropped his chin to his chest and raised big eyes. "Yes, ma'am, Mama. I'm *sowwy*."

Janyce nodded, then glanced toward Eli.

The little boy raised his head. "I'm *sowwy*, Mr. *Ewi*. Thank you for the *bwead*."

"You're welcome, young man." He caught Glory's look, but he didn't know the kid's name. With all his tremendous, God-given talent for speaking and memorizing the Word, his ability to remember names was practically negative.

Brandi sat between the two little girls, her smile bigger than he'd seen in months. Six months. She even nodded to something one of them said to her. Had she spoken? Said words?

His heart chugged a little slower. He hadn't heard a word from her since the funeral. Maybe he shouldn't have taken her to the service, but she wouldn't leave his side. She'd clung to him, screaming any time he tried to step away, as if she thought by staying near him, she could keep him from leaving her the way her mother had. For weeks, she'd even clutched his shirt in her sleep.

He accepted a bowl of soup and slice of bread and took them to his recliner. With the first bite, he marveled that restaurant soup could taste so good. And the crusty bread was so much like his grandmother's that he wondered how Halle had done it. Closing his eyes, he took a deep breath and slowly chewed. *That flavor makes me feel*—he tried to bring to mind a description of the emotion seeping through him—*whole*. The feeling was so good; he wanted to chow down his slice and grab another. Instead, he dipped his spoon in the soup and swallowed a savory bite before he put another piece of bread in his mouth. *Funny how just eating the bread, or maybe it was the fragrance of it, makes me feel loved, secure, as happy as if I could never do anything wrong.* Each time he took a bite of soup, he rewarded himself with bread. Finally, he gazed at the last bite, breathed deep so he could catch the sweet, yeasty goodness. *The bread completes me.* He rolled his eyes at the smarmy thought. *Good grief. I must have cabin fever.*

Glory caught the eye roll. Setting her bowl on the hearth, she got up off the floor and hop-stepped over the kids. "Would you come slice more bread? The kids are loving this stuff."

Only if you'll stay with me, and when I pet it and call it 'My Precious', then try to scarf all of it down, you'll slug me. He cleared his throat. "Sure. Glad to."

They walked together to the kitchen. At least he was getting used to not having electricity. He'd stopped flipping the switch each time he went into a room.

She gingerly pulled a loaf from the still warm oven and put it on the cutting board.

Eli grabbed the knife and started on the bread. *Dibs on the crumbs.*

"I really could have done this by myself." She

buttered each slice as he lovingly separated it from the loaf. "But I had an idea, and I wanted to see what you thought of it."

"Oookay..." He dragged out the word. Curiosity, a dangerous thing for a guy.

"Let's take Janyce and the kids to stay with Mrs. Jackson." Her face grew bright with the idea, her eyes shiny.

Her smile curved her lips and made him wonder what they would taste like if he kissed her. Then her words made contact with his brain, bringing the cranky woman he'd met earlier to mind. "She might be nice to those kids, but thirty minutes with the woman would probably make Janyce want to jump out the window. Or off a bridge."

"I don't think so. With the kids around, I really think Mrs. Jackson will be nice to everyone." She kept her face down, buttering the bread just right. "We've used her house before when an abused woman needed to hide from her spouse. She was great. Of course, the church helped with their living expenses."

"That's a good idea. There's probably not a man anywhere brave enough to take on Mrs. Jackson, no matter how bad he wants to get to his wife." He easily imagined Mrs. Jackson protecting a woman and her children from an abuser. "But would the church pay for Janyce's living expenses? You said she's not a member."

"I have a better idea." Picking up the bread platter, she turned, started out of the room, and tossed him a glance over her shoulder. "You need a new secretary at the church—the old one moved away last week—so Janyce can work for you."

3

Eli stared at the empty doorway. *I like to hand pick the people I surround myself with, especially my secretary. I know what I need. I know what kind of personality is easy for me to be around. The woman should work with me, for me, and through me. Sometimes she'll be the face of the church, its personality. I should choose the one who's best for me, not let the pianist do it.*

There were few businesses in town. A fast food place with some of the best barbeque he'd ever eaten, a full menu restaurant, a couple of offices, the weekly newspaper and Sparkle. In a small town like Jordan Valley, there weren't many opportunities.

A woman with three children and no support from her ex needed a job she could depend on, but was Janyce a trained secretary? Did she have church experience? As the head minister, he didn't have time— *Are you hearing yourself, buddy? That's the kind of thinking that landed you in this small town world.* He caught up with Glory in a couple of steps. "I'll agree on a trial basis. If it doesn't work out, no hard feelings."

Glory nodded.

"But who'll train her?"

"That's no problem. I worked as the church

secretary for a while, and I filled in when the last one couldn't be there. I'll train her." She didn't let the bread slip off the platter—he was ready to catch it if she did—as a smile tipped her mouth. She locked her gaze to his. "You have a deal."

She continued to hold his gaze, the hazel burning into him, making him feel as if she didn't want to move. Eli couldn't look away. The urge started in his gut, drew him closer without moving him, made him want to pull her to him so he could taste her lips, hold her there until he could feel the beat of her heart and she could feel his. *And ruin another woman's life?* Unable to break the gaze, he lifted his head and stepped back.

The spark in her eyes faded to…disappointment? If she knew him, though, she wouldn't be. If she really knew him, knew what went on in his head, she'd probably run screaming out of his house into the knee-deep snow.

He'd be right behind her if he could just get away.

The kids fell on the bread the same way he wanted to. Being a "responsible" adult, he only took one piece instead of scrambling for the entire tray. When the kids had their fill, they abandoned their food and started playing.

Glory gave Janyce a bright smile. "We have a great idea, Janyce."

Janyce looked a little leery, as if she'd already experienced some of Glory's bright ideas. She glanced at Star, who shrugged and shot Glory a questioning frown.

"I haven't talked to Star about it, but Preacher Eli

and I think it might be a good idea to take you to Mrs. Jackson's to stay until you can get on your feet." As she talked, her smile grew larger.

"Mrs. Jackson?" Janyce's forehead creased. "Oh, you mean the older woman who rides around town on a bike?"

Glory nodded. "You haven't lived here long, so you couldn't know her. She was a teacher here most of her life. The best teacher Jordan Valley ever had. She has a two-story home with several bedrooms over on Independence Street. She and her sister are in their late eighties and they're all alone."

Hoping to soften Glory's tirade a bit, Eli interrupted. "They really could use help taking care of that house and keeping the fire fed right now. It can't be easy for them. And I'll bet Mrs. Jackson would love your children. Isn't Zoey in kindergarten? Is she reading yet?" Eli was startled he remembered the little girl's name.

"No." Janyce dropped her gaze to the floor rather than meet his. "She's missed a lot of school this year."

Because you had to move before the rent came due? Or was she sick because you didn't have the money to feed her properly? He gritted his teeth and, for just a moment, he wished he could meet the father of her children and explain to the man why he should support them. And if the guy didn't understand his words, he'd love to tell him all about it in other ways...Eli squelched the thought. "I got a little better acquainted with Mrs. Jackson and her sister this morning. You'll love them both." *I hope.*

Janyce slowly nodded.

He only hoped that wild-bird-about-to-escape look would fade after she got used to him. "And....I was wondering if you've ever done any secretarial work."

"I worked in an insurance office a few years ago. I didn't do a lot of computer work, but I copied, filed, and mailed a lot."

Great. "Well, I need a secretary, so if you're interested, I'd be glad to let you give it a try."

She didn't answer for a long moment.

Had his...well, Glory's...job offer shocked her?

Finally, she took a wide-eyed breath, and shrugged one shoulder. "Sure. I'd love to."

~*~

Glory slid into the front seat of Eli's SUV, leaving Star and Janyce to situate the kids in the back. Star spent more time with the kids at daycare, so she'd easily be able to corral them. Glory glanced toward the rear of the car. Thank goodness for the third row of seats in the far back. Now all the kids could ride together, and Star could ride with Janyce in her car.

With everyone buckled in, Eli shifted into reverse, and after a little tire spinning, the car moved. "Do you think you should have called Mrs. Jackson first?"

A touch of panic fluttered through Glory. "Normally, I would have. But the phone lines are still down, and Mrs. Jackson and Miss Charlotte don't have cell phones." Much too quickly, before she could think of what to say to Mrs. Jackson, they turned into the former teacher's driveway.

Eli opened both doors on the driver's side, circled and opened the doors on the passengers' side. "Come on, lady. This is your show."

His aroma stayed with her, infusing her with visions of long sunny days spent lying in a field with nothing to do but be together. He held out his hand to help her.

Bolstering her courage, she slapped her freezing cold hand into his warm and much larger one, and just hoped the cold and heat together wouldn't cause a storm. At his tug, her toes tingled, but she swung her feet out the door anyway. If her legs wouldn't hold her, at least there was a crowd there to pick her up. And laugh at her.

And, knowing Star, who'd arrived right behind them and was already out of her car, she'd post pictures on social media so the world would know.

Somehow, even though the kids had all scrambled out of the car and were scampering in the snow, she was the first one to the front door. She rang the doorbell and, after what seemed like several hours, it squeaked open.

"You're back?" Mrs. Jackson wasn't smiling.

Glory might have called the look a scowl if she didn't know the woman. Could be, anyway. "Did you miss us?" Glory forced a grin.

"No." Mrs. Jackson looked past Glory, her eyes widening as her sloping mouth morphed into a smile. "Did you bring me company?" Her voice was lighter and brighter when she saw the kids.

"Yes, we did." Glory's grin became real.

Eli was suddenly there, his presence warming the space around him. He eased past and into the house while he focused on Mrs. Jackson. "This woman and her kids need a little help. A place to stay."

Mrs. Jackson's face transformed again, this time into a frown. Her mouth bunched, but she nodded and raised her voice. "Well, thank you for thinking of Sister and me! We were getting lonely here, just the two of us."

"Come on, guys." Eli didn't give her time to change her mind. "Mrs. Jackson wants to meet you."

The kids screamed and stampeded toward the door as if they were meeting a famous cartoon character in the flesh.

"Take off your boots before coming inside." Miss Charlotte's sweet voice was firm.

As one, the kids all stopped and tugged off their boots.

Janyce, her eyes cresting with tears, held Glory's attention. Pain tore through Glory's heart, nearly unbearable.

"Thank you. Oh, thank you," Janyce whispered in a trembling, ravaged voice.

Miss Charlotte came up behind Mrs. Jackson. "Why are y'all standing here like a flock of geese, too silly to shut out the cold?" The sweetness in her voice kept her words from sounding harsh. "The kids will probably like some cocoa. Would you drink some, too?"

"I would!" Star answered, and when she and

Janyce had tugged off their shoes, she grabbed Janyce and dragged her through the door.

Eli and Glory were close behind.

Miss Charlotte hurried out of the living room. Star and Janyce followed, asking if they could help. The kids, always restless, swarmed after them.

"Sit down," Mrs. Jackson barked as she sat in a wingback chair.

Glory, knowing it was futile to argue, obeyed. She chose the adjacent chair, and immediately wished she'd found a place a little farther away—New Zealand, maybe. At least there was a small table with several drawers separating their matching chairs.

~*~

Eli waited until Mrs. Jackson and Glory were seated, then stepping past a heavy coffee table, sat on the end of the couch nearest them. "Is this a problem, Mrs. Jackson? I guarantee the church will meet their living expenses until Janyce can make her own way." *Or I'll pay it myself.* Where had that thought come from? The question faded as something started burning in his chest. The sensation was familiar, but what was it? It had been so long since he'd done something right and known it was the right thing to do. Finally, he recognized the burn—determination.

"Oh, for pity's sake. I'm not worried about that." Mrs. Jackson frowned hard. "I'm just wondering if we need to watch out for an irate husband this time."

"You don't have to worry about that." Glory

tucked her leg under her.

Did she know how she looked, all curled up like a cat on a cushion? Cozy and relaxed and, well, approachable. Did women ever know? Eli's forced his thoughts back on the conversation.

"He abandoned them. Left one morning and they haven't heard from him since."

"That sounds familiar, doesn't it?" Mrs. Jackson raised one eyebrow before she shook her head. "Well, shoot. I was hoping I'd get to use my zapper."

"Your zapper?" Eli asked.

"Yes, my zapper. After that last go 'round with the abusive husband, I decided we needed some protection. So I made Sister drive me into Tulsa to buy me a cattle prod. You know, those things some ranchers use when they're working cattle? But it was too heavy and too long for me, so the clerk suggested that I check into stun guns."

He tried to imagine the frail looking old woman wielding a cattle prod on a drunk man. The image just wouldn't come.

"Did you get one?" Glory asked.

The old woman's eyes sparked with glee. "No. I bought two. And I keep them right here." She patted the table next to her.

"Have you had the occasion to use them on anyone?" Eli couldn't resist asking.

Mrs. Jackson curled one side of her mouth down as she shook her head. "I was hoping this would be my chance."

Glory leaned toward Mrs. Jackson, her face filled

with concern. "Don't you think you should put them away while the children are here?"

"Absolutely not. Children need boundaries. They need to know what they can do and what they can't." Mrs. Jackson lowered her voice. "Besides, it's a keyless locked Chinese table that Papa brought back from Chicago years ago. You have to know how to open it. They'll never find them, much less touch them."

And if you're attacked, will you remember how to open the table to get to them fast enough? "Couldn't you just use pepper spray?"

"We did, Brother Daniels. That man just kept coming. He grabbed Sister and was shaking her so hard, I thought he would break her bones." She folded her arms and sat back in the chair. "I had to conk him with Papa's door stop to get him to quit."

"You mean that little rubber thing you shove under a door stopped him?"

Mrs. Jackson closed her eyes and sighed. "Of course not. Papa was in World War One and he brought back a doorstop made out of iron that looked like the Eiffel Tower. We used it a lot before we had air conditioning, to keep the door open so we'd have a draft. But with the cooler, we haven't needed it so much anymore. It got kind of shoved behind the drape next to the door.

"He was yelling and shaking Sister, she was quoting scripture at him, and I was slapping him, trying to get him to quit. He shoved my old body off toward the wall, and when he did, I struck my foot on the Tower. Well, he'd gone back to hurting my sister, so I just picked it up and conked him on the head." The look of pride in her eyes was unmistakable.

He couldn't blame her, either. "I'll bet that slowed him down."

"Yes, it did." A small smile spread across her face. "Slowed him so much, he still wasn't conscious when the ambulance got here to take him to the hospital."

Eli clamped down on the amusement roiling inside him. "What did the police say?"

"Boyd Hubbard was the policeman who came. I tell you, if I'd known what an idiot he would grow into when I had him in first grade, I'd have flunked him for another year or two." She rolled her eyes heavenward with an irritated sigh. "He told me I might have done real damage to the man. Said the man's family could file a lawsuit against me. I told him to go back to the police station and look up the Make My Day Law. That jerk should have been glad I didn't have a gun."

"Do you still have the Eiffel Tower?" Eli asked, fascinated with the thought of this woman conking anyone.

"Yes, I do." She nodded. "Boyd took it for evidence, but I told him if I didn't get it back, I'd be the one filing suit. It is a little bent, though."

Eli actually chuckled, delighted with her story. Had he known any women in his big church that could have stopped an abusive husband? No. But then, he hadn't known women who would have put themselves in that situation. "Do you remember what scripture Miss Charlotte quoted?"

Mrs. Jackson chuckled. "It's a funny thing,

preacher. The kids staying with us had trouble sleeping because they were scared of the dark, and who could blame them? So Charlotte had been reading the sixteenth Psalm to them for their bedtime story. When their daddy tracked them down and broke in, he grabbed her, and she said all she could think was that eighth verse, *I keep my eyes always on the Lord. With Him at my right hand, I will not be shaken.* When she got to that last part, she was yelling."

Eli suppressed the laughter that was threatening to shake him.

The kids piled back into the room, followed immediately by the adults.

"Be careful, Star. Don't spill it." Miss Charlotte hurried across the living room and, opening the fireplace screen, she took the poker, raked some of the coals to the front, then turned the concreted hook out into the room.

"What are you doing, Sister?" Mrs. Jackson demanded. "The gas stove in the kitchen is still working."

Mrs. Jackson's bark didn't seem to faze Miss Charlotte. "The children have never seen anyone cook in a fireplace, so we're going to show them what it was like in the early days before anyone had electricity or gas."

"Well, be careful of that iron hook. As long as that fire's been burning, it'll be hotter than blazes." Apparently, Mrs. Jackson didn't believe in letting anyone else have the last word.

Miss Charlotte's face grew pink from the warmth

of the fire. "Yes, Sister. I know."

When Star got to the fireplace, she gingerly hung the pot of milk on the hook.

Miss Charlotte used the poker to swing it back over the coals.

Janyce set a tray filled with mugs, a ladle and a long-handled wooden spoon on the coffee table and handed the spoon to Miss Charlotte while Star settled the children where they could watch without getting in the way. Miss Charlotte used the spoon to stir the cocoa, then moved back a little from the fire.

"How come you don't put the pot over the fire? Wouldn't the cocoa get warm faster?" Zoey asked.

"You see, children, the heat rises from the coals to slowly warm all the milk. If Sister had put it over the fire, the milk near the heat would warm so fast, it would scorch it, but the rest would still be cold." Mrs. Jackson got out of her chair and crossed to the children, where she slowly got down on her knees next to them. "Has anyone ever tasted scorched cocoa?"

The kids, including Brandi, all shook their heads.

Eli's heart pounded as his daughter interacted with the others. Hoping she'd respond, he used one of his wife's expressions. "I have! It's gross-me-out-the-door!"

All the kids laughed. Even his daughter.

"And drinking a lot of scorched cocoa might make us sick. And that would just be too bad because we don't have a *nurse* who can take care of us." Mrs. Jackson pinned Glory with her gaze.

Had Glory aspired to be in the medical profession

when she was younger? Changed her mind? Decided it wasn't for her? No shame in that. He knew lots of people who didn't have the stomach to do that kind of thing.

Before he could ask, Miss Charlotte changed the subject. "The thing you want to do besides not scorch it is to keep the milk from coming to a boil. That could curdle it."

"What's curdle?" Zoey asked.

"It's little lumps in the milk. It would be kind of like having cottage cheese in your hot chocolate."

"Ew."

Miss Charlotte smiled at Zoey's response. "So you must watch for the steam to start rising, kind of like it is, and tiny bubbles to form around the edge of the pot, kind of like they are, and you know it's about ready."

The kids edged a little closer to look into the pot.

"Star, would you run back into the kitchen and get a hot pad?"

Mrs. Jackson grumbled about people who always forgot *something*.

Miss Charlotte used the poker to ease the hook around, so the pot was away from the heat.

"Let me get that for you." Eli took the potholder from Star, then moved past Miss Charlotte, fitted the pad around the wire, and started to lift the pot. Despite his care, his index finger touched the hot metal hook. "Ow!" He quickly let go. The pot settled back in place.

Glory was instantly beside him, dragging him out the front door. She grabbed a handful of snow and stuck his hand in it. "It'll probably blister."

The burning stopped enough for him to notice her eyes were mostly brown with flecks of green, circled by a rim of green around the iris. She must have noticed his attention had strayed to her because after packing another handful of snow around his finger, she opened the door. "Mrs. Jackson, could you get us a bowl, please?"

Maybe she was getting chilly out there without a coat, or she didn't enjoy being ogled by a minister. Or maybe she could see into his heart and was smart enough not to like what she saw.

Mrs. Jackson was quickly there with the bowl, which Glory scooped full of loose snow, and put his whole hand in.

"Well, at least you haven't forgotten everything you learned." Mrs. Jackson sniffed. "Why don't you come back into the house before you turn into icicles?"

Glory's jaw muscles flexed twice and, finally, she nodded. "Let's take this to the kitchen."

He shifted his hand to bury his injured finger deeper in the slush and then followed her inside.

Brandi ran to him and grabbed him around the leg.

He lifted his hand out to hug her but the pain nearly made him cry out. He deep-sixed the hug and settled for an elbow-around-her-neck embrace. "I'm fine, Brandi. Really."

She captured his gaze and held it for a heartbeat. The first time she'd done that in forever. After a last look at his hand, she ran back to play with the two little girls.

A soft smile played around Glory's mouth.

Eli followed through a dining room and, turning the corner, found himself in an old fashioned kitchen. He set the bowl on the counter next to the sink, careful to keep his finger well covered. "What was Mrs. Jackson talking about?"

Glory opened a couple of drawers and pulled out a towel with "Monday" embroidered on it. "It's no secret. Everyone in town knows—I'm a quitter, can't-hack-it Glory."

"That's ridiculous. You have a successful daycare, you've played the piano for the church for years, and you have your own ministry of keeping children in need free of charge." He made his tone sincere. "That doesn't sound like a quitter to me."

She sighed and lifted her gaze to meet his. "You just don't know. I went to college on a scholarship, and earned a BSN. I had big plans to be a pediatric nurse. I graduated and passed the boards, so I'm a registered nurse. I even worked for a time in a hospital in Oklahoma City in the peds unit. But I couldn't handle it. The hours were long, and often I had to work a double shift because they wouldn't hire enough help. And they wouldn't buy the equipment we needed. The patients suffered, Eli. All the hospital cared about was their bottom line. I dreaded going to work, so I made up excuses, illness, anything so I wouldn't have to go.

"Finally, I quit and came home. I told people it was because I missed Jordan Valley and my family, and I did, but the real reason was, I couldn't handle it." Her voice dropped low. She didn't cry, even though most women would have after an admission like that. In fact, her eyes stayed totally dry. She looked exhausted as if she'd lived the story, repeated it, and been punished for it too many times.

He couldn't cry for her, he'd used up his tears after Miranda and Jeremiah. And Brandi.

She glanced at the door as if she thought they should go back with the others.

He wasn't quite ready. "How much trouble will it be for you to help train Janyce to work at the church?"

She blinked a couple of times at the sudden change of subject. "It depends on how good her office skills are. I don't know—"

"No, I mean will it take you away from the daycare too much? Do you need to be there, handling the kids?"

Her smile came after the shine returned to her eyes. "Most of the time I don't deal with the children themselves. I'm on the administrative end of the business. I hire the help and train them, plan the meals and snacks, order supplies, and plan the crafts and games. If a child is hurt or ill, I oversee their care."

He smiled at her admission. "Then you do use your education on the job."

"It's bandages and ice, mostly. The kind of first aid kids learn in high school." She glanced toward the door. "Now may I ask you a question?"

He nodded, but he didn't want her to. He knew what was coming.

Her smile was as absent as help on work day. "Why doesn't Brandi speak?"

Pat answers, platitudes he'd used for the last six months, flooded his mind. *She's shy, she'll talk when she gets used to being around you, she only speaks when no one else is around, must not have anything to say,* and the always popular, *I wish there were more of us like that.* His heart twisted, panging hard as the truth fought to come out. The panging stopped so suddenly, he wondered if his heart had stopped, too. Or maybe God had spoken. *Why not?* He nearly snorted. *Because a man whose daughter won't even talk to him isn't much of a man. A minister who can't even help his own child is a zero. It's proof that at heart, I am really not good enough.* He drew a ragged breath. "The doctors have some name for it, but it's trauma from the wreck. From seeing her mother and uncle die."

Tears brimmed Glory's eyes. "She was in it?" Her whisper was soft.

"Her safety seat did its job that day. The car looked like a balled up piece of foil, except for where Brandi sat, in the middle of the back seat." His eyes were wet, too. That hadn't happened since he cried himself dry. One funeral, two caskets, bearing two of the people he'd valued most in the world. "Unfortunately, it took several hours to cut them from the wreck."

She took an unsteady breath. "I'm so sorry."

He pulled his hand from the melted snow. There, on the side was a white blister about the size of a dime. The pain returned, but he let it drill into his finger. The burning was easier than reliving the torment he'd suffered since that day. The knowledge of how he'd failed, and then failed to realize he had failed until it was all over. "A drunk driver hit them late one night near Laredo, Texas. Took me several hours to get there from Dallas, and by the time I did Miranda and Jeremiah were gone."

"Laredo?"

Once more, lies, old friends that they were, came to mind. *They were visiting relatives. Going to pick up a friend. Checking out a place for a women's retreat. Shopping for a used car.* The ones he'd told himself, some he'd spewed for the congregation and some he hadn't. But the truth had come out, ugly as it was humiliating, and he'd been fired. Oh, they'd kept it quiet and allowed him to act as if he'd chosen to leave, but they'd given him the boot as surely as if he'd burned down the church and roasted wieners over the flames.

As hard as it was to meet her gaze with the memory of his failure returning so strong, taking a breath became next to impossible. He raised his head to find her gaze and lifted his shoulders in a shrug.

And even that was a lie.

He knew why Miranda and Jeremiah had gone to Laredo. How could he not know? It was as plain as day, and as big as his ego. He'd failed his wife, and she'd turned to his brother. And the three of them had paid the price.

"Stop it!" Glory grabbed his hand and jerked his thumb away from the blister.

He didn't realize he'd been pressing so hard.

"No matter what you heard, if you break the blister, it won't feel any better, and it's liable to get infected."

He gave her a thumbs-up as he hoped to lighten his own mood. "Maybe you're not such a failure as a nurse after all."

4

Glory went out to the sidewalk in front of the daycare and walked toward the church. With the electricity back on—thank You, Jesus!—she and Star had been able to go home the evening before. Star had spent the night at their childhood home, rather than going to her apartment in town.

Earlier today, the daycare had filled with parents heading back to work in the city, but for some reason, the daycare help hadn't been as punctual.

After sorting through keys, Glory fitted one in the lock and went into the church through the kitchen. Janyce had remembered to make coffee. Taking a deep breath of the rich aroma, Glory poured a cup and then entered the church's office suite from the rear, just outside Eli's office.

He'd turned his desk so it faced his office door. She could see his dark hair as he bent over his work and his broad, broad shoulders. His arms filled his sweater sleeves, a tight fit. He must have been a weightlifter. A blush rose on Glory's face as she recalled the quick glimpse she'd seen when he'd removed his shirt in the laundry room. She'd looked down quickly but hadn't missed the tattoos.

When word of his hot looks and desirable marital status got out, their single—and not so single—female attendee numbers would probably explode. Trouble was, people who came for a reason like that weren't likely to stay after he left. Their commitment would be to Eli, not the Lord.

She knew beyond doubt that Eli wouldn't be staying, even if Jordan Valley was the absolute best small town in the world. And it didn't matter what he'd said when they hired him about needing a place where he could raise his daughter, find peace for himself, do the Lord's work, and build His church. She gave him two years, max—just one of the reasons she'd voted against hiring the man. She'd bet her stethoscope on it—if she knew where it was.

She enjoyed the play of muscles in his shoulders as he reached for a book on the shelf behind him. Almost against her will, she was drawn farther into his office. Wanting to circle the desk to stand near him, close enough to smell his scent, feel the heat that emanated from him, she forced herself into one of two chairs in front of his desk and held on for dear life. "Sorry, I'm later than I intended. Brandi and the other kids made it to daycare on time this morning, but Star's help was late."

He nodded, staring at his desk for a moment before lifting his gaze toward the door. "She'll need help."

She'd known Janyce was inexperienced. "Most of us do when we're new at a job. What did you tell her to do?"

"I wasn't sure what to tell her, so I said just to answer the phone until you got here."

"Oh. My." Laughter bloomed, tickling its way up until she couldn't hold it back. "Didn't you have a secretary at the church in Texas?"

"Yeah. But she'd been there a long time. She told *me* what to do."

"Well, let's start at the beginning. Do you have your sermon for Sunday?"

He reached into the top basket on his desk and pulled out a file. "I thought you'd have a presentation program here, so I printed the outline and highlighted the scriptures."

"Good. I'll need it to prepare the song service. I'll give Janyce a list of the scriptures and the title for the bulletin." She opened the folder, focusing on the title." *Finding Humility in Today's World.*

Humility? Had she read that? "W-what's your scripture reference?"

"Micah 6:8. 'He has shown you, O mortal, what is good. And what does the LORD require of you? To act justly and to love mercy and to *walk humbly with your God.*'" He cleared his throat as if he'd just swallowed something that hadn't quite gone down. "Not a scripture that's used often."

Glory nodded. *At least it'll be different.*

~*~

An hour later, Eli sat on the front pew.

Glory, her eyes shut, played a very simple version

of *Sweet Hour of Prayer*. She played it without the extra flourishes she'd added to the music the Sunday before, almost like a beginning piano student. A very proficient one. When she played the last note, she held it until the sounded faded completely. Finally opening her eyes, her attention landed on him, warming him. Her gaze held his for a long moment before drifting to the cup in his hand. "You aren't supposed to be in here with that."

He glanced at the coffee he'd nearly forgotten as he listened to the simple perfection of the song. "Sorry. I missed that communiqué."

She tilted her head to one side. "The carpet is kind of new, and we're hoping to keep it looking good for as long as possible."

Dark red carpet, like so many churches he'd visited. "I'll remember from now on."

She picked up her phone, lying on the piano next to the music stand, and glanced at the screen. "Oh, I've got to go. I have a Chamber lunch in ten minutes at Sparkle. I'm president, so I have to be there. I'll work on the music this afternoon." She slid off the bench.

He stood as she came off the platform. "You're in the Chamber of Commerce?"

She nodded, glancing toward the door.

"How do you find the time?"

She tossed him a self-deprecating smile. "I can't seem to be uninvolved. Jordan Valley is the best small town in the world, and we have to keep it that way. So I serve on the Chamber board because I want to make it even better."

He waited a moment to see if she would invite him along. She didn't. "Must be a great way to get to know people in the community." *Take me with you. In Dallas, I would have had a special invitation. Actually, I did.*

She was about to leave, her mind obviously on where she was going and what she'd be doing as she read something on her phone. A list, maybe? Notes? But her gaze flickered up, back to her phone, and then settled on him. His words had reached her.

Her look made him glad he'd wandered in to listen to her play.

Her eyes widened while a frown dented the area between her brows. "Would you like to go with me?"

Oh, yeah! "Go with you?" He paused as if considering it. *Faker.* "Yeah. I'd like that."

Back in his office, he put on his coat.

Glory and Janyce were speaking in the outer room, but their words were indistinct. When he stepped into the outer office, he didn't have to be told what the discussion was.

"There really should be someone here in the office." Glory sounded rushed. "Because it's the church policy to have someone here during office hours. We're walking over, but I'll send a Sparkle Special back with Eli."

Janyce's eyes brightened.

Glory walked out the door.

Eli murmured goodbye and escaped with a prayer of thanks. In his experience, whiners didn't wind down quickly or quietly. He caught up with Glory.

She glanced at him before fixing her attention on

the slippery sidewalk. "We could drive, but it's only a couple of blocks, and when the Chamber meeting is there, the parking is awful."

At least she'd admitted to something that wasn't perfect in her town. He could add a few things, such as their lack of culture, the closest coffee shop was an easy forty or fifty miles away, and their only sports teams were little league and school associated, and not very good at that. But the elderly sisters who'd taken in Janyce and her kids came to mind, making him admit—only to himself, of course—that at least the people in this town cared about one another. "No problem. As warm as it is today, I don't mind walking."

One of Glory's eyebrow dipped low. "I have to stay after the luncheon for a board meeting."

"I think I can find my way back." He didn't try to hide his teasing grin.

They rounded a corner and in a few steps were on Main Street, just a few doors from the shop.

Her mouth flashed a bright smile just before she pushed open the door. The handshaking started as Glory introduced him around. He should have warned her about how awful he was at remembering names. Maybe if he concentrated on occupations...

As Glory's guest, he was seated at a table with her; a woman who sold real estate and spoke in a high baby-talk voice; and a slender, dark-haired man who owned the local newspaper.

While Halle set plates of Mexican casserole, salad, and a crescent roll in front of them, the editor said, "I'd like to run a piece about you on our church page, if you don't mind."

Before Eli could answer, the real estate woman clapped her hands. "Oh, I just love it when you have real people stories. You should do that *alla* the time."

The editor cleared his throat, blinking a couple of times as his face went blank. After a moment, the man grinned. "Thank you, Sharon. I appreciate that." He turned to Eli with a slight shrug. "You know, most people enjoy knowing a little bit about who's running their church. They might not have attended since high school, but it's still *their* church, which makes you *their* preacher, so they want to know."

Eli thought about his request. Should he grant the interview, or should he ask the church board first? And if he did talk to the man, he'd have to be careful about what he said. No one really wanted to know the flawed side of their pastor, no matter what they said about love, forgiveness, and support.

When everyone was served, a man at another table stood. "Let's bow our heads." He proceeded to say grace for the meal.

After a chorus of amens, Eli leaned toward Glory so he could speak softly. "That was unusual."

"The blessing?" she guessed correctly.

"Yeah. I'm surprised you can still get away with it."

The editor, obviously listening, leaned toward him. "The Chamber here in Jordan Valley, at least, is a private organization, even though it's open to pretty much anyone who wants to join. So, we pray, and we've never had anyone complain."

"I hope you can keep it that way."

The subject changed to a small manufacturing firm that apparently had considered moving to town.

Eli concentrated on his lunch. The casserole tasted homemade. In fact, it tasted better than some of the home cooking he'd experienced in his years of church dinners.

Soon, a man at the next table caught Eli's attention. "Hey, Brother Daniels. Aren't you from Dallas? Rumor has it the owner of the Outlaws Football Team was a member of your church. Did you know him?"

"Yes, Stan Martin was a member of our church. He even took me to a few of the games." Of course, Stan attended only occasionally, and Eli hadn't known the man well, but he didn't share that information or the fact that the few times he'd attended games, he'd felt as if he put a damper on the festivities in Stan's box. He'd stopped going.

He'd had other famous, and infamous, members in his congregation. Minor movie stars, a senator, and a big-time author all had their names on the roll there. He'd even met them a time or two. He'd save those stories for another time though because sadly, he'd never been able to make regular attendees out of them.

~*~

When Glory got back to the church, Eli called her to his office.

"How did your meeting go?"

"Fine. Seems like we can never get out in under an hour, though." She turned toward the door.

"Wait! Where are you going?"

"To the sanctuary. I don't have the song service ready for Sunday, yet. Did you need something?"

His smile turned mischievous. "No. Just wondered."

She held the pages of Eli's sermon close as she hurried to the piano, anxiety roiling in her belly. She usually had a several days to prepare, but this time she'd have to hustle . She hated feeling rushed. Sliding onto the piano stool, she placed the sermon on the music rack and read the fairly straightforward outline with scriptures noted along the way.

She considered the words printed there, and the words he'd probably use to fill the gaps. She picked up the Bible she kept on the piano, put it in her lap and turned to Psalm 36. Shoulders warming as she read, her muscles loosened. The words on the pages blurred as tears filled her eyes. Blinking them away, she let her gaze wander down the page.

"Your love, LORD, reaches to the heavens, your faithfulness to the skies. Your righteousness is like the highest mountains, your justice like the great deep."

Keeping the Bible in her lap, she played the song they'd sung so often she knew it by heart. After a few moments, the song changed, and she let it flow from singing about God's love to His majesty and holiness. She played for several minutes and then took her phone from her pocket and called the members of the worship team and confirmed that they would be there early Sunday morning for a time of prayer and practice before Sunday School. Sometime later, when the service was as ready as she could make it, she stretched her back to get the kinks out, put on her jacket, and headed for the door.

"All through?"

She couldn't see Eli easily, but his voice rumbled in the semi-darkness of the empty hallway. Rather than startle her, as a voice out of nowhere normally did, it gave the lowlight of the corridor a velvety excitement and made her glad to be alive. Was that voice the reason he'd decided to become a minister? It certainly ministered to her tired back. Of course, she could never tell him that. His gaze burned into her, making her go weak in the knees. How did he do that? Did everyone he met feel as if he were seeing all the way to their heart? He really couldn't, though, could he? She cleared her throat before she dared to speak. "I thought you'd gone home hours ago when Janyce did."

He walked closer, the twilight from the front windows reaching him now. The way his sweater pulled across his shoulders made her wonder how it would feel to lean on him. Just having him beside her as she walked into the darkness made her feel protected.

"I'm sorry about the lateness of the hour, but I needed to finish up some things. I hope your sister won't be mad."

"We tell most parents that if they can't pick up their children by six, look for them at the police station, so you're good."

"Do people want to leave their kids at all hours?" He held the door for her, followed her out and reached into his pocket for the keys.

"Some of them think that, since the daycare is part of our home, we should jump at the chance to keep their precious babies all night after we've had them all day." She laughed, hoping to soften her words. "Not gonna happen." Pulling her jacket close, she stayed near as he locked the door, but only because the key was often hard to turn. It had nothing to do with the heat emanating from him or the way he made her feel like a puddle of hot caramel. *Keep telling yourself that.*

He slid the keys into his pocket, his gaze moving back to her. "Since it's so late, why don't you let Brandi and me take you to dinner to make up for it?"

"I'm afraid if you take me to dinner, you'll have to take my sister, too. It's my right to cook."

"I meant you and your sister. After all, I've inconvenienced both of you tonight." He turned and she thought for a moment he would touch her elbow or slide his hand along the small of her waist, but he didn't. The emptiness of disappointment echoed inside her.

"I'd love to go out." Star was thrilled at the suggestion. She helped Brandi put on her coat and then slipped into her own. "We're ready to leave this place, right, Brandi?"

Eli smiled at his daughter.

They walked to the church and got into his car. He drove to Blackjack House on the far side of town, the only full-menu restaurant in Jordan Valley.

When they were seated, Christie, the owner, brought a coloring page and a small box of crayons for Brandi, and handed the adults their menus.

Brandi grabbed a purple crayon and went to work on the pony on her page.

"A purple horse?" Eli asked, glancing Brandi. "Did you ever see a purple horse, baby?"

"I did," Glory answered, pasting on a bright smile in case Brandi looked at her. She didn't. "I love purple horses, especially when they fly."

"Me, too." Star's smile wasn't bright. She clamped her mouth shut, a sure sign she wasn't happy about something. Her brows settled in a frown, too.

Glory's heart sank. *Now what?*

Star glared at Glory for a moment before turning to the little girl. "Hey, Brandi? Did you see the big fish tank over there? Did you know there's a mermaid in it?"

Brandi looked up from the page, which she'd colored entirely purple.

"Want to see if she looks like the one in the movie?" Star lifted her lips in a fake smile.

Brandi nodded and looked at her father.

"Sure. Go ahead." He closed the menu and kept his gaze on his daughter. "But don't go anywhere else."

As soon as Brandi was out of earshot, Star glanced at Glory and then fixed her gaze on Eli. "Brandi does not speak. Ever." She ground out the words. "I know this is the first time you've had her come to daycare, and I agree she might be shy."

"I know," Eli said.

"All day, whether she was playing with the other kids or all by herself, she didn't utter one word." Star went on as if he hadn't spoken.

"I know."

"When we first played bear hunt, you know, when the kids repeat what I say, I thought she didn't repeat me because she didn't know the game. But I watched her today and tried to draw her out, spent time with her one-on-one and in small groups, and she never said one syllable."

Eli looked weary, but he nodded.

"Eli, do you think she could have been molested?" Star asked.

Shock stiffened Glory's back. That thought hadn't even crossed her mind.

Star gave her a look and then turned back to Eli. "I've heard that molested kids sometimes quit talking to keep from telling anyone because they're threatened or they don't want to get that person in trouble. Do you think it could be that?"

"Brandi doesn't talk, but she hasn't been molested." Eli's voice rumbled deep in his chest.

From the look on his face, Glory wouldn't have been surprised to see tears in his eyes and on his face, but there were none.

"She hasn't spoken in six months, not since they cut her out of the car wreck when her mother died."

Star gasped softly. "Oh, I'm sorry."

Glory's throat thickened as tears built inside her. Even though she knew what happened, it still broke her heart.

Eli kept his gaze on his daughter as another little girl about the same size scampered to her. "The drunk that hit them was driving one of those big pickup trucks that looks like it's on steroids with a brush guard on the front. Our car looked like a balled up piece of aluminum foil. I was told it took several hours to cut Brandi out, but she wasn't hurt except for some slight bruising and a couple of scratches. The emergency workers said it looked as though there was a protective box around my baby, protecting her."

"Angels." The word slipped out, a whisper, more of a prayer, really, that should have been lost in the talk and clatter of the diner, but both Star and Eli stared at Glory as if waiting for her to continue. Glory's heart thudded inside, as it always did when she heard about a weird thing God had done. "Don't you believe in angels, Eli?"

"Of course, I believe in them. I'm a minister of the Gospel, after all. I've just never seen one in action."

Something about the way he said the last sentence made her think it was a slick answer he'd used before.

Star laid her hand on his forearm for a moment, stood, and went over to the aquarium where the other little girl was trying to get Brandi to talk.

"Maybe you have seen an angel or evidence of one." Glory watched his face, trying to read his thoughts. "I hope you aren't Balaam."

Eli's gaze sliced to her face with a glance so sharp, she wondered if he'd cut her.

"A preacher who doesn't remember who Balaam

was?" she teased. "You know, the story in the Old Testament?"

"I remember." His smile was sad as he bowed his head, almost as if he were praying. "Miranda, my wife, wanted to write children's stories. She loved telling Brandi that one. She called it the story of two donkeys because, she said, Balaam was as stubborn as a mule." Rather than brighten at the happy memory, his face darkened.

"Is that where you'd heard the story of David and Goliath the way you told it the other night?"

He nodded, swallowing before he answered. "Miranda did it better."

"Did she ever sell any of her stories?"

"No. She never really had time to try. Life was extremely busy in Dallas with all the things the minister has to be involved in." He shrugged, the movement slow and careful as if his burdens weighed a thousand pounds. The sadness left his face, and something else claimed it. Shame?

She softened her voice. "You know, Eli, if she'd wanted to write bad enough, she'd have made the time."

He shook his head in such a slight movement, she wondered if he realized he was doing it. "No, *you* don't understand. She couldn't have because I wouldn't let her." Shoving back his chair, he abruptly stood. "I need to wash my hands. Excuse me."

As he walked away, every woman in the room watched him go. Including her.

Sighing, she slid down a little in her seat, rested

her head against her chair back. *Way to win friends and influence people.*

By the time Christie brought their dinners, Eli was back at the table with his clean hands. Star and Brandi were back, too. And, yes, most of the women in the place had turned their chairs so they could easily watch Eli.

As they were eating, a group of women came in together, several of whom looked vaguely familiar, and were seated near the front of the restaurant. The women were obviously on a girls' night out and having a good time. Before long, they sent over a frilly pink drink to Eli and lifted their glasses to him when Christie delivered it and pointed them out. "Welcome to Jordan Valley!" one of them called, and they all giggled like little girls.

Eli gave them an easy smile and, without looking a bit embarrassed, called, "Thank you." Lifting the drink in a return salute, he took a sip. His eyes widened, his mouth pursed as he blinked hard.

Glory thought he would spit the mouthful back into the glass.

Finally, he closed his eyes and swallowed, set that glass down, and picked up his water and took a long drink. "What is that?" He cleared his throat.

"It looks like Christie's special strawberry lemonade. Super sweet, and guaranteed to keep a child hyped up for hours." Glory picked up one of her shrimp, dipped it in the tartar sauce. "I think they sent you a message, preacher boy. Sweets for the sweet."

He shuddered. "Are you sure Christie doesn't

have some kind of deal with a local dentist? She creates the cavities, and he fills them?"

"Could be," Glory answered. "And I wouldn't be surprised to see several of those women in church Sunday morning."

"And, hopefully, they'll hear what I say."

"I hope so, too," she murmured.

"Riiight..." Star chuckled.

When the check came, Eli left the cash to cover it plus a nice tip. And as they were leaving, he gave Glory a slight nudge before stopping at the table full of women. "Ladies, thank you for the lemonade. I'm Eli Daniels, pastor of the Jordan Valley Community Christian Church here in town. I'd like to issue each of you a personal invitation to visit us this Sunday."

"I'm one of your members, Brother Eli." The woman had heavily streaked hair, and batted her eyes as she talked.

Glory didn't recognize her.

"I'm glad to meet you, then." He gave the woman an artificial smile.

Glory had noticed during Chamber that when he was meeting new people, his grin looked as plastic as a kid's toy—practiced and perfect, showing his very straight and even teeth, and bringing out a dimple low in his right cheek. But the sparkle that should have been in his eyes was absent. It was the kind of smile a politician would wear. If he ever smiled at her like that, she might have to smack him.

Halle walked in.

Eli's smile became real as they turned to leave.

"It's the woman who makes the best bread in the world."

"Hi, guys!" Halle hugged each of them in turn, including Eli, then she stooped to say hi to Brandi.

Brandi looked back at the woman, her eyes wide.

Halle's brows lowered a fraction of an inch when Brandi didn't answer, but rather than remark on her silence, she turned to Star. "I was going to call you. Can you bake a Decadent Devil's Food Cake for me for tomorrow night by six?"

"Sure. What's the occasion?"

"The gaming group is having their monthly meeting in the shop tomorrow night. They love your cake."

"I'll have it to you in the afternoon."

When they walked back outside, the night was blue from the vapor lights illuminating the parking lot.

Star took Brandi's hand, and they practiced skipping.

Eli glanced down at Glory. "Decadent Devil's Food Cake?"

"Yeah. If you've never had it, you're in for a real treat next time we have a potluck dinner at the church. I'm not sure how she makes it, but it's a chocolate cake with chocolate chips, caramel, and toffee, and she tops it with chocolate whipped cream."

"That sounds delicious." He touched her elbow as she stepped over a nearly melted pile of snow. "I can't wait."

5

As Eli steered out of the parking lot, careful to miss the leftover snow piles that hadn't quite melted in the warmth of the day, Star touched his shoulder.

"Can you drop me at Halle's store?"

Startled, he glanced in the rear-view mirror. "You aren't baking that cake for her tonight, are you?"

Her chuckle was barely audible. "No. I live in one of the apartments over the shop."

"All right." He drove a couple of blocks, turned onto Main Street and, because Halle's store was on the other side of the street, he shot a U in the same spot as he had the day after the big snow.

"If the police see you do that, they'll give you a ticket." Glory murmured so softly, he doubted Star could have heard it.

He waited until Star was out of the car and going into the recessed door before he turned to Glory. With only the lights from the dash and one from the streetlamp half a block away, she looked shadowed, mysterious and beautiful.

She glanced over her shoulder, looking for traffic. "It's clear."

When she turned back and caught him watching

her, she colored so deeply he could see it in the dimness. "What?" she said.

He hesitated another moment, then kept his voice low. "You told me to make that exact turn just a few days ago."

The color in her face deepened even more and, strangely enough, he liked it.

"But-but no one was out that day, and when the roads are like that, you can get away with almost anything but speeding or being intentionally reckless because the police don't pull too many people over when it's that cold. I don't know why that is. Maybe they don't want to have to stand out in the frigid weather and listen to excuses. I'll have to ask Dal sometime." She stopped talking as suddenly as if she'd hit a wall.

Eli had never heard her chatter on with her sentences all running together. Could the easy-going-always-in-control Miss Glory Matthews be flustered? He smiled as he glanced for traffic over his shoulder. He backed out of the parking place, shifted into gear, and started back down Main, still enjoying the afterglow of her word flood. *What would it take to fluster her again?* He drove past his driveway and pulled into the daycare.

"You didn't have to bring me down here. I could walk from next door." Her voice sounded raspy, as if she'd caught a cold in the last few moments.

"If I didn't, my mother would reach down from heaven to smack me. Hard." He put on his parking brake, got out and walked around the car to open her door, but by the time he got there, she was standing on the sidewalk. He opened the rear door and stuck his head inside. "I'll be right back, Brandi baby, as soon as I walk Miss Glory inside."

"No, there's no need for that, Eli. I'm perfectly capable— "

"I'm walking you in." Standing toe to toe with her, he looked into her face.

Her cheeks darkened again. Defiance flashed briefly in her eyes but quickly left. "All right." Turning abruptly, she started toward the house.

He easily caught up with her and slid his hand to the small of her back. Something about being that close and touching her just there made him stand a little taller.

At the door, she pulled out a jangle of keys big enough to be used as a weapon, singled out one, and stuck it in the lock without looking at him. "Well, goodnight."

He nearly chuckled as he realized she wanted him to leave. Immediately. She got the door open, turned, blocked the entrance and hiked her chin just a bit. "Good. Night."

She's the one. I'll care for her, and she'll care for me. She'll be a pleasure to spend my time thinking about, talking to and just being around. Surprise sparked somewhere in his chest at his wayward thoughts. Instead of obeying her unspoken command to go, he nodded, put his hand to the door over her head and walked in. She had no choice but to take several backward steps in a silent dance unless she tried a body block, and he had a feeling she didn't want to do that.

In the light from the ceiling of the big, toy filled room, her cheeks were rosy pink, her eyes wide and her lips parted as if she were about to ask him what he was doing.

So he kissed her. *What am I doing? This was only supposed to be a quick peck. A friend kiss.* It had been so long since he'd kissed and been kissed. At her quick rush of breath, he stepped closer, slipped his arm around her waist and pulled her to him. She smelled of something light and sweet, like springtime flowers. Her lips softened as she warmed to him, and the awe of it filled him, stripped time away and nearly turned him to stone.

And then her hands were on his shoulders, and he knew he had to stop, but he didn't want to. He loved having her in his arms and the way his heart pounded as if he were alive again. He hadn't been touched, really touched, by anyone in six long and lonely months. Or was it longer?

Guilt struck hard right in the vitals, causing his stomach to tense and his chest to grow heavy.

What had he done? Miranda would never kiss anyone again. She wouldn't kiss or make more babies or see the baby they'd made together grow up, go to school, and someday get married, and it was because of him. And her baby waited in the car right now while he kissed another woman. What kind of man was he?

He kept his eyes closed and prayed he could remember Glory's kiss—the warmth, the softness, the feeling that for a moment, someone cared for him.

Maybe later, when the loneliness returned, he could remember it and he wouldn't feel so lost. He lifted his face and looked into her beautiful hazel eyes.

Even her ears had turned red now, her face nearly glowing.

He dropped the kiss he'd first intended on her nose, stepped back and was finally able to draw a breath.

She didn't say a word. She just stared at him as if wondering whether they'd broken a Commandment.

Darned if he could find the power to speak, either. Finally, he forced a breathless, "Goodnight," and fled, his heart chugging as if he'd just escaped with his life.

Or his sanity.

~*~

He couldn't get that kiss or Glory out of his mind while he got Brandi ready for bed, or while he took off his own clothes. The diametrically opposed twins of guilt and pleasure held on like two dogs with a single bone between them. When sleep finally claimed him, he even dreamed about it. The feelings were still fighting on Sunday morning while the worship team sang, and it seemed the one named guilt was growing bigger and meaner every moment. He shouldn't have kissed her.

The piano mic Glory used wasn't close enough to her mouth for him to hear her above the others, but after a couple of songs, she pulled it close. "On beautiful mornings like this, when the sun is shining and the snow about gone, I can't keep from thinking about the flowers stirring underground, getting ready to pop out and shout the glory of the Lord. I remember a little neighborhood Bible School I attended when I was about eight. It was a week long and there were four of us students and two teachers, who were about ten."

The congregation chuckled.

"We had lessons and crafts, but the main thing the two girls wanted us to do that week was learn Psalm 100. It was the first thing I ever memorized and I didn't think I could do it. But I did, and I remember it to this day. 'Make a joyful noise unto the Lord, all ye lands. Serve the Lord with gladness. Come before His presence with singing. Know ye that the Lord, He is God. It is He that hath made us and not we ourselves. We are His people, the sheep of His pasture. Enter into His gates with thanksgiving and His courts with praise. Be thankful unto Him and bless His name! For the Lord is good.'" Her voice cracked and grew husky. "'His mercy is everlasting and His truth endureth to all generations.'"

Words flashed on the projection screen, and the worship team started singing the song she'd been quietly playing while she quoted the old memory verse. Although it was hard to hear what she played with the organ booming, she kept her right hand moving while she lifted her left hand and put it on her chest. Soon, both hands were over her heart, and she was singing with her eyes closed and head bowed. Then the organ stopped along with the guitars and drums, and the entire congregation sang the last verse without music.

Beautiful. And it seemed as if most of the people had joined Glory in real worship.

Using his velvety voice and God given talent, Eli shared one of his best received sermons, which he'd written while in Texas.

Eight people joined the church that morning—five women, two youths, and one man, whose wife apparently dragged him with her. *And so it begins.*

After the closing song, he stood at the entry and shook hands with the people as they left.

When only the stragglers were left, Glory wandered up to stand beside him, bumping him lightly with her shoulder. "Catch everybody's name, did you?" Her teasing gaze sparkled. "You know, they'll expect you to remember them next week."

Maybe the time was right to make the call that would get him out of there. For sure, he needed to be in a huge church far away where recalling names wasn't expected, and people were too busy to get very well acquainted with him. The last thing he wanted was for anyone to learn all about him, especially Glory.

"If everyone had names like yours and your sibling, it'd be much easier," he murmured just before taking the hand of an older man.

The man said his name—which immediately slipped out of Eli's mind—complimented the sermon, and the strength of Eli's easy-for-even-an-old-man-to-hear voice—which confirmed he was the loud mouth his mother always told him he was—and left.

Eli and Glory were alone except for Brandi, who ignored them as she played with small cars in the foyer.

"All right, what was the man's name who left by himself a few moments ago?"

Eli tried to bring the man's face to mind, but it wouldn't come. "What is this, a test?" He opened the glass door and adjusted the settings so it would open only from the inside. He turned back.

Glory stood in his way, challenging him. "If you get to know the people in your congregation, it'll be easier to remember their names."

Eli's stomach grew tense. The part of the ministry he despised—getting to know people meant letting them know him. He shrugged one shoulder. He'd tried every memory trick he'd ever read about and still couldn't remember names, probably because he didn't really want to. In a big congregation, it didn't matter that much. He belonged in a church where a man couldn't be expected to remember every name, where assistant ministers handled what he didn't do well, so he could focus on what he did do well, and no one— absolutely no one—knew what was truly in his heart. For that, he was truly thankful .

He gave her his best, we're-in-this-together smile. "Sorry. God just didn't give me that gift." That answer usually worked. But he hadn't counted on her tenacity and stubbornness.

"When you really know about a person, care about him, you'll remember his name." Her voice was quiet but firm. "The man who left by himself is named

Singleton. Mark Singleton. His wife died about a year ago because she had surgery, and while she was in the hospital, she got a MRSA infection. They'd been married nearly fifty years."

Fifty years was a long time to love one woman. Be with her every day and night, live with her through gains and losses, joys and sorrows. Get to know her and, worse, let her get to know you. Your weaknesses. Your inabilities. Your sin. Losing a woman who'd been with you for a lifetime and who loved you anyway could break a man. That much he did know.

The man's face came back to him — a scar bisecting his upper lip that had healed unevenly, a smile that disappeared so completely one wondered if had been there at all, and hooded eyes shadowed with soul-deep sadness. Was there guilt behind Mr. Singleton's disappearing smile that matched Eli's own? "That's horrible. Did they have kids?"

She nodded. "Two daughters, grown and moved away. They both wanted him to live with them, but he wouldn't go. Here's the thing about Mr. Singleton. He was a hit and miss member for years, but when his wife was in the hospital for all those weeks before she died, he became more regular. Never missed Sunday school or Sunday worship or Wednesday night. When Mrs. Singleton died, I was afraid he'd quit coming to church altogether. I mean, he'd asked for prayers for her, and ended most Sundays in the prayer room, praying for her on his knees with one elder or another. And then she died. The first Sunday after her funeral, you know what he did?"

The loss of a wife, whether of fifty years or seven, hit too close to home, bringing back his own failures—full blown. He hated to remember, because at times like these, the pain he worked to dam up hit hard. It filled him with grief so terrible, it stole the strength from his muscles, and nearly melted his bones. Unable to speak, Eli shook his head.

"He spoke to the congregation. Thanked them for their prayers, and thanked God for his wife's healing. He told us she was healed and perfect and waiting for him in Heaven. And he's never gone back to his sometimes attendance at all. In fact, he teaches one of our Sunday School classes now."

Automatic, velvet-tongued replies came to his mind. *God moves in mysterious ways. We never know the working of the Lord.* He decided to go with always safe scripture. That proves that "All things work for the good...." The words died in his throat. Disappointment filled her eyes as if she'd given him a beautiful gift and he'd thrown it in the dirt. He ditched the rest of the scripture he'd started to spout and looked deep inside. "What I mean is, it's amazing the difference it can make knowing *about* God, and really *knowing* Him like a kid knows his dad. I have a feeling Mr. Singleton fell in love with God, and had no desire to go back to the other way of life. It's much too lonely. And cold." *I know about lonely.* Why did his voice suddenly sound all crackly, as if he were about to cry?

Brandi fitted her little hand in his and looked up at him, her eyes wide.

Relief blew through him like a cold breeze at the

reprieve. Grateful, he blinked hard and knelt to put his arm around her. "Ready to go home, baby?"

She nodded, put her arm around his neck and spontaneously hugged him for the first time in half a year.

He nearly bawled.

~*~

Glory pulled up the official daycare stationary on her computer and made a face at the gingerbread people that boogied across the top of the page. Mom had picked the name of the daycare—Gingerbread Giggles—all those years ago. "My daycare, my decision, my name," she always answered when Glory suggested any kind of change, such as "Gee-Gee's" or simply "Giggles."

To be honest, she didn't mind the dancing gingerbread people or the name.

Centered at the top of the stationary she posted "Menu for the week" in bold letters and then looked at the local grocery store ad. Chicken breasts were on sale, so the kids would get their favorite—crispy oven baked chicken strips with ketchup, green beans, and fruit cocktail gelatin cups. On the menu, she wrote, "Chicken Pecks, Giggle Beans and Jiggle Fruit." Underneath, in parentheses and a smaller font, she noted what it really was. Tuesday, they'd have whole wheat spaghetti, so she wrote, "Wiggle Worms."

With the menu finished, she printed out two dozen copies so each parent could have one and she could post them in the kitchen as well as several other strategic locations. After picking up the copies from the printer, she circled her desk and headed toward the door.

When the phone rang, she reached across her desk to answer it. "Gingerbread Giggles, may I help you?"

"Good morning."

Tension zinged through her. No mistaking, the deep voice on the phone belonged to Eli. The rumbling quality went with his muscular body perfectly. His voice and looks had probably distracted people from looking beneath the surface of his life. There was more to the man than he let people know. Maybe more than he knew.

He'd taken their job, although the salary was nothing compared to what he must have received in Dallas. Their congregation in Oklahoma was much, much smaller with almost no potential to grow. Even if everyone in the town of Jordan Valley became a member, it still wouldn't be half the membership in the huge church he'd headed.

With those vast differences, she had a feeling he hadn't waited on the Lord to lead him. And that kiss the other night—had the Lord led him to do that? Had He sent the tingles that were taking over her body even now? She drew a much needed, if shaky, breath. "Hello?"

"You sound out of breath. Did you have to run to catch the phone?"

No, you snatched the air out of my lungs. "Just busy. What can I do for you?"

He hesitated as if waiting for her to say more. But she couldn't talk. She could barely breathe. Finally, he said, "Just calling to check on my girl."

Her face flashed hot, the heat quickly consuming her entire body. Weak in the knees, she collapsed on the old couch before the haze cleared from her brain enough to remember Brandi in the big room with the other children. "Um, I'm not with them right now, but I was there for morning songs, and she was fine. Is there a problem?"

"No. She didn't eat much this morning, so I thought she might have a sore throat or something."

The sigh that followed his words tugged at her heart. Obviously, he hadn't planned to raise his daughter alone, hadn't prepared for it. He'd thought his wife would be by his side forever, but now he was on his own. When he married again—and a man who looked like he did would almost certainly marry again—would it be for love or because he needed someone to raise his daughter? The thought slowed her pounding heart, her body cooled a bit and her brain started to function. "I'm preparing the menu for the rest of the week. I'll check on her when I post it."

"I'd appreciate it." After a long moment, he disconnected the call.

That intimate tone, spoken so softly right into her ear, tried to steal her breath again. She really needed to learn to ignore whatever it was making her emotions fluctuate.

Your heart, maybe?

The words came to her mind out of nowhere. She

glanced around to see that yes, she was alone in the room. It couldn't be God speaking, could it? She crossed her arms to ward off the chill that swept over her. After all, her name wasn't Moses, and there were no burning bushes anywhere around. She hoped. Maybe she should check. She slipped the phone into her pocket. Had she eaten her breakfast? Because inside, she had a giant hole the size of the Grand Canyon.

"We're home!" Aunt Rosemary's familiar voice echoed through the hall.

"Star, Glory! We're back!" Mom's tones were happy.

Relief eased something deep inside of Glory. It was always good to have them home and know they were safe.

The fuss the children made grew to a low roar.

Glory rushed to meet them. She stepped into the playroom.

Mom and Aunt Rosemary nearly smothered her with hugs and gardenia perfume.

"Oh, sweetheart! We came as soon as we heard!"

Being taller than her mother by about five inches didn't make it easy to lay her head on the maternal shoulder, but for some reason, hugs didn't feel complete until she'd laid it there for at least a few seconds. "How was the cruise?" She lifted her head, her neck snapping lightly as she did.

"Tell us all about him!" Mom ignored Glory's question and linked arms with her.

Aunt Rosemary grabbed her other arm.

They all but dragged Glory back to the office. They pulled her down between them to sit on the old couch.

"Tell!" Mom demanded.

"Tell what?"

Aunt Rosemary, a year to the day younger than her mother, which made them Irish twins, looked a lot like her, except instead of a smooth, bobbed hairdo like Mom's, she wore her graying locks in a long, straight ponytail that laid across her shoulder. "We heard the new minister is here and that he's got the body of Hercules and the face of Adonis."

And the mouth of an angel. Glory kept her own mouth firmly closed on that subject. "Mom, his wife died only half a year ago."

Aunt Rosemary looked sad for a few moments. "But you're not getting any younger, you know, Glory. Didn't you turn thirty this year? It's high time you found someone."

"Aunt Rosemary, I'm thirty-three."

"If you're thirty-three, Star's thirty, isn't she?" Rosemary asked.

"You're both single." Mom took the conversational ball again. "I'm positive one of my girls will be perfect for this man of God!"

"Mom, he's a big city boy. Grew up in Kansas City, and lived several years in Dallas. I think he's just here to try to get back on his feet, then he'll probably head for someplace like Los Angeles, Chicago, or New York, where he can build an even bigger congregation than that mega church he had in Texas." She stood and grabbed her bottle of water from her desk and drank deeply before turning to sit in the chair across from the couch.

"But you got used to Oklahoma City when you lived there, didn't you? You could get used to Los—"

"No. I *never* got used to the city. I was never comfortable or happy when I lived there. I couldn't breathe right, I couldn't go out by myself, and even though I went to the same church every Sunday when I wasn't working, I never saw the same person twice. I hated it!"

"But it would be different if you were married to the minister." The ball was in Aunt Rosemary's court now. "You'd have dinners with the board members, teach a Sunday School class or, even better, sit with him while he taught one. You'd get to know people."

"I don't think he's ready for someone new in his life, and his daughter isn't either. She's in the next room, and having lost her mother—"

"Oooh," Mom and Rosemary said in unison. Both jumped to their feet, grabbed her arms, and hauled Glory into the next room.

~*~

Again, they flanked her.

"Which one is she?" Mom whispered from the side of her mouth.

"Her name is Brandi." Glory called the children, giving Star and her helper some respite. While she made the introductions, she put one hand on the Brandi's shoulder and slid it to the back of her neck before touching her forehead. No fever, thank goodness. "I think these ladies have a new story they want to read you," she told the children.

"Is it about a princess?" Zoey asked.

"I want a *thory* about magic." Liam didn't like being outdone by his sister.

Her mother and aunt smiled brightly, and stepped right in.

"This story is better than a princess or a magic story," Mom answered. "It's a mystery. Can you say mys-ter-y?"

The pair started their story. Mom read while Rosemary took notes, then they switched. If the kids started to lose interest, the note taker would scribble furiously, and when the kids leaned forward, nearly begging for more, she made a note, also. The story finished, they asked the children questions.

The kids answered happily, sometimes jumping out of their seats and sometimes shrugging their answers.

Then Mom singled out Brandi. "Which was your favorite part?"

Brandi stared at her, so Aunt Rosemary tried. "Brandi, what part did you like best? When the sisters hid in the trashcans? When they were in the canoe?"

Brandi's eyes grew wider, but that was the only change in her. Finally, fisting her hands between her knees, she ducked her head.

Aunt Rosemary asked someone else.

With lunch to serve, Glory didn't have time to answer her mother's questions about Brandi. After the kids had gone outside to play, Glory busied herself with cleaning up. But even though she had to wipe down the tables and return the unused napkins to the kitchen for the cook to put away, they waited.

"We're headed out to have our lunch now," Mom announced. "Let's go see Halle."

"I need to run—"

"No." Mom's voice was a stern as it ever got. "Glory, we're eating lunch first. Then you can take care of whatever."

~*~

When they were seated at Sparkle and had ordered salads, Mom took control of the conversation. "What's wrong with Brandi? Why doesn't she speak?"

"It is disturbing," Rosemary picked up the verbal tennis racket.

"According to Eli, she was in the wreck that killed her mother and uncle. She hasn't spoken since."

Mom frowned. "You mean something like that can make a little girl stop talking for six months?"

"Even longer."

"Maybe she's autistic." Aunt Rosemary said, sympathy brimming in her eyes.

"I don't think so." *Please, Halle, bring the salads. And hurry!* "She interacts with the other kids and plays with them. Being touched or held doesn't seem to bother her, either."

Rosemary had her cell phone out, reading something. "It's called selective mutism, and can be caused by trauma or shock, but is most often caused by social anxiety."

Mom's eyes glinted while her mouth curved into a knowing smile—what Glory had come to think of as her story embryo look. "Where'd you read that, Rosie?"

"Online. I love my phone."

"Bookmark it. We might need—"

"Hello, ladies."

Mom might have finished her sentence, but Glory didn't hear her. Eli's voice, smooth and delicious as melted chocolate overwhelmed her auditory senses.

Mom smiled while Aunt Rosemary tucked her hair more firmly behind her ears.

"Glory, I don't think I've met your girlfriends." He stood politely behind the empty chair.

Memories of his kiss buzzed inside her. She warmed as she remembered the texture of his lips on hers. Reminding herself to breathe slowly—how embarrassing would it be to hyperventilate and fall out of her chair?—she forced the corners of her lips upward. "Eli, this is my mother, Ginger Matthews, and my Aunt Rosemary."

"You must be the original Matthews girls I keep hearing about around town." His low chuckle sent a warm tingle down Glory's spine. "It's good to meet you."

"Sit down, Eli," Mom invited. "We've met your daughter already. It's nice to meet you, too."

"I called in my sandwich to go," he answered as he pulled out the chair opposite Glory.

"Halle won't mind if you decide to eat in." Rosemary gave him her brightest smile.. "Now, tell us all about yourself."

He laughed as if he thought her mom and aunt truly delightful.

They were charming and funny. Sometimes, she forgot that. She glanced toward Halle, who was too busy preparing lunches to look up. She had only one helper for the lunch rush, but this one looked like someone new. Maybe Glory should go over and introduce herself. Find out if Halle needed any assistance since a new person often didn't see things that an experienced person noticed. And since Glory had pitched in more than a few times when Halle was shorthanded, Halle might appreciate it.

But when she focused once more on their table, Mom had her hand on Eli's arm with her head tossed back, laughing at something he'd said. Maybe she'd better stay. No telling what her mom and aunt would ask him if she wasn't there. Or what they might tell.

Halle finally brought their salads. "You didn't tell me what dressing you wanted, so I used my new recipe. It's an apple juice vinaigrette with maple syrup and Dijon mustard. I think you'll like it."

"You didn't ask for ranch?" Eli asked.

"No." Halle, the sisters, and Glory answered in perfect harmony.

He raised one eyebrow and turned his head a bit, so his attention was completely on her, making her forget how to breathe. "But I thought ranch dressing was the house dressing of Oklahoma."

"We're changing that image one salad at a time," Halle answered and, with a flip of her ponytail, went back to the kitchen.

"So, Pastor Eli, Glory tells us your daughter doesn't speak. Have you taken her to a doctor about it?" Mom asked.

Glory almost choked but Eli answered smoothly, as if he'd been asked the question many times.

"Yes, I've taken her to a doctor."

"What did he say?" Aunt Rosemary asked.

"He said she'll talk again when she's ready." He picked up his sandwich again.

"You should get a second opinion," Mom said.

He turned so he could focus directly on her mother and lifted one side of his mouth in a knowing smile.

How could her mother breathe with him looking into her, practically seeing through her like that? Glory drew a ragged breath.

"What makes you think I haven't?"

Seemingly unaffected by his scrutiny, Mom gave him a bright smile. "And what did your second opinion say?"

"The same as the first and third. 'She'll talk when she's ready.'"

Mom had always been one to fix whatever was broken and fix it now. Maybe that was why the day after their dad abandoned them, Mom had filed for divorce, and changed her name and the names of her children to Matthews, her maiden name.

Pressure built inside Glory like a balloon blown

too full of air. She couldn't just sit there and listen to them talk about Brandi. "I've got to go." Oops. She'd interrupted Mom mid-word.

All eyes turned to her.

Mom's mouth was open as if Glory had snatched the word right out of it.

She really needed to listen better when Mom was talking.

She thought wildly about her day, trying to remember something she truly needed to do. "I-I almost forgot my Bible study." She took a drink of water and then waved for Halle to bring her a to-go box. "I need to get back and work on it. It's right after school with the high school girls."

Eli nodded, wrapped up his sandwich and put it back in the bag. "I'll go with you. I'd like to meet your high school Bible study group."

She started to suggest that he stay, but she took pity on him. "All right."

After putting her salad in a carry-out container and telling her mom and aunt goodbye, they left.

"Is there really a Bible study today?"

"Of course. Would I lie to my mother and my pastor at the same time?"

"You mean, you'd rather lie to us separately?" He wasn't smiling, but his dimple showed in his cheek—something that happened, she'd noticed, when he didn't want to smile.

"Of course," she answered on a chuckle. "So there are fewer people to remember my actual words."

~*~

"That's your strategy?" He raised one eyebrow higher than the other. "What are you studying?"

What would he do if she returned the kiss he'd given her, and gave it back right there on the street? Would he respond or draw back in embarrassment? Would his lips feel as warm? So softly firm that she'd want to keep on kissing him as she had the other night?

He was looking at her expectantly. Had he asked her a question? Something she needed to do. Oh, yes. The high school Bible study. Had he asked about the subject? Was there a subject they were studying? There had to be. They couldn't just sit and look at the cover, could they? She thought hard, trying to remember something — anything — about it. What was wrong with her? "L-Luke 7, studying about the woman with the alabaster box."

He stopped and stared at her, a frown puckering his forehead. "Teenagers?"

What? She wanted to ask, but instead, she nodded. "Middle school and high school girls."

His frown grew deeper. "And their parents agreed to it?"

"I didn't ask them if it was OK, but they know what we're studying. I'm sure they'd speak up if they didn't approve." What was his problem? *"Why?"*

"Because the woman with the alabaster box 'had led a sinful life.' That most likely means she'd made her living as a prostitute, as women often had to do at that time in history. Do you really think it's appropriate to be teaching young girls lessons about prosti—" At her chuckle, he stopped speaking.

"First, Eli, we didn't go into what it means to make a living as a prostitute. And second, middle school girls these days probably know more about sex than I do." She shrugged as his frown grew even deeper. "We have sex education, TV and movies, and the Internet to thank for that."

Jaw muscles flexed as he turned on his heel and started once more toward the church. "Yet another vote for home schooling."

6

Eli opened his Bible and tried to put Glory out of his mind. But Glory had a totally different take on the story than most he'd heard. Instead of the woman being forgiven as she washed Jesus's feet with her tears, she suggested the woman was forgiven previously, and her tears were because she'd found that in following Christ, she could be victorious. Where'd she get that part of the story?

While he might not agree with her, he wasn't about to argue the point. It wasn't a salvation issue, and if Glory were to become upset and quit, teaching those teenaged girls could fall to him until they found a replacement. And even if it was just temporary, there was *no way* he could spend an entire hour every week listening to their chatter and giggling and silliness, and not want to plug up his ears with concrete.

The hardest part of the afternoon had been the girls just a few years older than Brandi. The two younger ones still had that plump baby look, even though they had mascara making their lashes stiff and straight and garish colors on their eyelids. Had they left the house looking like that or had they added the blinding color after they'd escaped the parents?

But what really bothered him was their talk. They spoke with the assurance and knowledge of kids more experienced than they should be at their age. And some of the subjects they whispered about, and naïvely thought he and Glory couldn't hear, were very adult.

He'd escaped as soon as he could gracefully exit.

"Are you OK?" Glory asked, standing just inside his office door. The corners of her lips curled suspiciously as she spoke. Laughing?

"What do you mean?" So what if little girls flustered him? That crew would have flustered anyone not used to teen girls. "I just had to get back to work on my sermon."

She sat in one of the chairs. "I-I really think I need to share with you about these girls." All signs of her smile disappeared.

"What's there to know?"

"Remember Roni, the blonde with long, straight hair? She's a foster child."

He thought of the girl with the pouty mouth and seeking eyes.

"She's been in the system since she was small and has gone through everything foster children"—she lowered her gaze to the floor before focusing on him again—"suffer. She's extremely…mature for her age, if you know what I mean. And having you there, a young, good looking adult male, must have stirred up something inside her. She wanted your attention."

"Yeah. Well, she got it." At every lull in the lesson, the girl had tried to start disturbingly provocative conversations. "Is she still in foster care?"

"Yes. But she's with a good Christian family now. Hopefully, they can help her before she's on her own and making totally self-destructive choices." Closing her eyes, she shook her head.

"Well, I won't be asking Roni to babysit Brandi anytime soon." Finally, he tracked down a bit of humor in the afternoon. "No matter what she offered me as compensation."

"Are you kidding me?" Glory's eyes flew open. "Did she…?"

"When I was leaving, Roni said she was cold and needed to get her coat. She stopped near me."

Glory caught her breath. "I thought she was saying goodbye."

Roni knew how to work everyone, it seemed. "Oh, she was, but she had an invitation along with it."

"Oh, dear." Tears brightened Glory's eyes. "My heart hurts for her. She thinks the only thing that makes her worthy of anyone's attention is sex. Do you want to talk to her or her foster parents ab—"

"No!" The word exploded from his mouth. He did not want to talk to a pre-pubescent sex kitten about anything, much less the invitation she'd given him. If he ever had to repeat what she'd said… He nearly heaved at the thought. "If you want to talk to them, fine. But I'm staying far away."

"She has a hole in her heart she's trying to fill. Humans all crave love, but I think because of her past, she doesn't know what real love is. She thinks it's physical, something you earn. And she's right at the age that can really hurt her."

"Maybe you should sneak an agape love message into your Bible study."

"That would be almost as good as sticking a small bandage on a gushing wound. Maybe we should attack with all guns blazing." His face must have shown his puzzlement because she flipped her hands and caught her breath in excitement. "Don't you have a sermon or sermon series about love? You have to. All preachers do, don't they? Why don't you find it, freshen it up, and hit the church with it?" In her excitement, her eyes sparkled, and her face grew rosy—over God's Word.

Go figure. Oh, there was a time when the Word had delighted him, too, but that was a lifetime ago. He missed that feeling. Ached for it.

The gleam in her eyes made him wonder if her enthusiasm was communicable. If he rounded his desk to get closer to her, maybe even kissed her, could he catch her exhilaration? He nearly snorted out loud. *Right, Daniels. Love for God isn't like a cold or the flu.*

Before he could finish the thought, she came around the desk and sat in the chair she'd dragged there a few days before, and which he hadn't bothered to move back. "Not too long ago, Roni sent an inappropriate picture of herself to a boy's cell phone. His mother nearly had a heart attack when she saw it."

"I can imagine."

"God is the answer to her problem, but she doesn't know it." Her eyes blazing, she grabbed his wrist. "You know it, Eli. If you look at every problem in the world, at its very core is a lack of love. Of God."

Enjoying her rant, he nodded but kept his mouth

shut. He didn't want her to stop. He liked having her hand warming his forearm, her fingers gripping him as if she didn't want to let go.

"That's what people don't understand. The reason we're here is God's love. To revel in it, enjoy it, and share it with others." Holding his gaze with hers, she gave his arm a shake with each of the last four words. After a silent moment, her gaze drifted to her hand. Her tight grip shifted and started to ease.

Unwilling to lose their connection, he covered her hand with his and then slowly eased his palm along her arm to her elbow. As gently as he could, he pulled her toward him and, heart stampeding, he kissed her lips, which somehow fit his perfectly. His head filled with her light, gentle scent, causing his heart to stutter.

She broke the kiss but kept her eyes closed as if she were testing the air for something. Then, as if she'd heard a sudden sound, her eyes flashed open and, as she glanced around, her face flooded with color.

And without another word, she lunged out of the chair and all but ran out of the room as if the devil were after her.

Maybe he was.

~*~

Eli entered the church sanctuary where Glory had escaped to after his kiss. Smart girl. Leaning against the grand piano, he spread out his sermon. "Glory? I've decided to preach a series on love. The first week, we'll have an overview of God's love throughout the Bible, then we'll focus on different portions. Here are the scriptures and the outline." He named two or three passages. "And the last one is 1 John 4:8—Whoever does not love does not know God, *God is love.*"

Glory quoted the last three words in unison with him. She played a few notes on the piano.

He imagined the pews all filled to capacity. "We all desire love, we know God is love, and, we all need love. Therefore, all we really need is God." *If only that were true.*

"You know, most people really don't get that. If they did, life would be so much better. For everyone."

"Everyone?" He thought of his research thesis. He'd worked long hours over it, staying in the library every night until they practically threw him out, and Miranda told him she'd forgotten his name. "Statistics tell us only so many people in America will ever go to church, Glory, so everyone doesn't figure in. I don't want to get off the subject here because we really do need to finish, but believe me, false religions, cults, and anything-goes Christianity accounts for a percentage of people who do go to church. With those fantasy religions eating up part of that statistic, there are only so many people left."

Bowing her head, she stopped with her finger on one note and held it there until the sound faded. Lifting her hand, she settled it in her lap and looked him full in the face. "God doesn't read statistics."

Edginess filled his gut, straightening him. He tapped his papers together. "Of course not. But I'm talking about reality here. Facts. We can break them down to numbers here in Jordan Valley. A portion of the people here will never darken the door of any church, and of those who do, some would never walk into a church like ours, so that means we can only hope to reach the rest. Why beat ourselves up trying?"

She gazed at him for a long moment without speaking. Her look heightened the agitation filling his gut. Finally, she shook her head. "Here's what I think. If we work as if everything depends on us, and pray as if everything depends on God, He'll handle the rest."

"I've seen that bumper sticker, too," he snapped. As anger filtered in, it relieved some of his anxiety, his feeling that somehow his words proved him a failure. "I'm talking about the real world. We have to realize that we can't win everyone, not even here."

"And I'm talking about True Reality." Her voice grew lighter as a soft smile curved her mouth and brightened her eyes. "The kind that can't be seen or counted or figured on a calculator. The kind that spoke the universe into existence."

Sometimes he wondered if, after God spoke the universe into existence and created everything, He hadn't just backed off to see what would happen. Or maybe it was just in Eli's life where God had backed off. Not that he could blame Him.

~*~

Glory had just finished setting up the last play center at the daycare when she noticed Mom watching her. "Morning, Ginger-Peach." She grinned at her mother who looked beautiful and dressed up, even wearing a button-down shirt and jeans.

Her mother waited as Glory straightened and moved to her side.

"Did you need something, Mom?"

"Yes." Her mother spoke in a low tone, as if the children were inside trying to hear her, instead of outside having fun. "Have you considered using play therapy?"

"For a play center?" She glanced around the big room at the areas she'd put together. An art station with crayons and watercolors, a music station with kazoos, oatmeal box drums, and other home-made instruments, a builder station with plastic and wood blocks, and a puzzle station. "Play therapy? For the entire bunch of kids? No. I have thought about science experiments this summer, though. A tadpole or two and maybe some easy, non-explosive chemical reactions."

Her mother rolled her eyes as she folded her arms. "I'm talking about Brandi. Have you tried using play therapy? Helping her speak again?"

"Mom, I'm sure Eli took her to the best doctors in Dallas. And I'm not qualified—"

"Qualified?" Her mother's voice arced high. "Even though you've put the knowledge to little or no use, I sent you to college to be a nurse. Now is your chance to use what you know."

"Mom, I had a full scholarship. Remember? And I used my education for nearly a year in Oklahoma City. Besides, I didn't specialize in childhood psychological problems. Only physical ones."

"Oh, pooh. Brandi doesn't have a psychological problem. She just doesn't talk." Mom waved away the idea as if fanning a gnat, and filled the air with her sweet fragrance. "Why don't you get those old puppets out and see if she'd like to play with them? I'll bet she'd love Princess Precious."

"Princess Precious..." Glory bit back a smile.

"That's right." Mom's laughter was low. "I've been reading up on the subject, and I think she might draw Brandi out."

It took several very long minutes in the storage room to find the container labeled puppets. With a quick peek inside, Glory straightened with the huge box in her arms. "Let's take it back to the big room. The dust in here is choking me."

When they went back into the playroom, the kids who'd apparently had enough of sunshine and chilly ears swarmed them. Funny how children thought every unopened box had a treasure in it. This time, they were right.

Glory had the kiddos sit on the floor as she pulled out the puppets one at a time.

The figures were a little frazzled looking and smelled of cedar. Glory laid them on a low, child-height table. Forgetting they were supposed to sit, the girls were soon hopping up and down with excitement, but the boys got bored after a few moments and ran to the building block play area.

"Can I hold the princess doll?" Sophie asked.

"I want one," Zoey squealed in time with her

jumps.

Brandi just stared at the toys, longing in her eyes.

"These aren't dolls." Her mother knelt behind the low table. "These are puppets. Look, we can make them talk."

The girls watched wide-eyed as the princess, with the aid of Mom's hand, magically moved her mouth. "Hello, little girl," Mom said to Sophie.

"Hi." Sophie sounded a little shy.

Mom made the puppet look at Zoey. "Hello, little girl."

"Hello!" Zoey squealed, bouncing up and down.

"Hello, Brandi."

Brandi smiled at the doll, but didn't speak.

"Brandi, my name is Princess Precious. Can you say hi to me? I want to play with you."

Brandi's smile melted as she stared at the puppet.

"Anyway, that's how they work." Taking Princess Precious off her hand, Mom put the toy back on the table. "Maybe Glory can show you more later. But be careful with them. They're old."

"We will," Zoey and Sophie answered in unison while Brandi nodded.

Glory motioned the girls closer. They scampered around the table where she sat back on her heels. She handed each one a puppet, which they held as if they were made of spun glass. Taking the princess for herself, the best way to avoid a tug-of-war battle, she showed the girls how to put the toys on their hands and work their mouths. While Sophie and Zoey made the dolls' heads nod but not talk, Brandi didn't even try to put on the puppet.

Janyce came to the door to pick up her girls and their brother, Liam, who was busy building a snap-together block tower.

Sophie gently put down her puppet. "Tomorrow I get to play with Princess Precious," she said, her voice firm.

"Me, too!" Zoey shrilled.

"Let's go, kids." Janyce sounded tired. "I still have to pick up pizza for dinner."

While their mother bundled them into their coats, Zoey rushed over and gave Glory a quick kiss on the cheek. "Bye!"

When they were gone, the room seemed almost empty. A couple of the boys were playing with trucks while Star picked up blocks.

Brandi walked around the table near Glory and pointed to the princess puppet.

Glory picked it up.

Brandi stretched out one finger to touch the puppet's sparkly crown.

"Would you like to hold Princess Precious?"

Brandi's eyes grew wide, and she nodded.

Glory sat on the floor so Brandi could perch in her lap. "There you go, Princess Precious." Glory guided Brandi's little fingers inside the puppet so she could make it talk. Glory leaned to the side to see Brandi's face. "Do you like the princess, Brandi?"

Eyes sparkling like the sun, Brandi turned to Glory. The child made the puppet's mouth open and close several times. While she made the puppet work, her smile spread so wide, it looked as if it might tear her face in half. "Yes." Brandi whispered the word.

To Glory, it seemed as if she'd shouted and the sound reverberated, echoing off the Rocky Mountains and rolling back at them. *Yes!* Glory's heart raced with excitement as energy filled her limbs. She wanted to jump up and shout, *Brandi spoke!* Instead, she tried to think of something to ask Brandi to get her to speak again. "Would you like to have a crown like Princess Precious's?"

Brandi's shrug and the following nod dampened Glory's enthusiasm a bit. The four-year-old turned the puppet over to pick at the fraying rick-rack on her skirt. "Would you like to show the puppet to your daddy?"

Without looking up, Brandi slowly shook her head.

"I have an idea." Glory leaned toward Brandi as if taking her in her confidence. "We can make a play. It'll be a secret, just you and me and Zoey and Sophie. We'll all learn our parts, and then we'll have a puppet show and stage it for everyone."

Brandi stared at Glory. Maybe Brandi thought she'd lost her mind. Maybe the girl had the right idea. Had Brandi really spoken? Or had she imagined the child speaking because she wanted it so badly for Brandi and Eli? *Do you want it for them or because you just want to be a hero? To get Eli's attention and show Mom and Rosemary that you aren't a failure.* Deep sadness filtered in with the thought. *Oh, please, Lord, don't let me be that selfish.*

"What's up, guys?" Star carried the basket of blocks to the storage shelf and came back to the table covered with puppets. "Oh, wow! Bad Boy Roy. How've you been, guy?" She picked up one of the puppets, so named because one of his eyebrows had fallen off, was glued back on crooked, and the dimple next to his mouth had come unstitched, which made him look as if he were smirking.

"I'm fine. How are you?" Star answered for Roy with a screechy sound Glory thought of as Star's puppet voice. Then Star made Roy turn and look at Princess Precious. "Yo! Princy Baby! How ya' doin?'"

They waited, but the princess didn't answer, and her mouth didn't move.

Brandi let Princess Precious droop from her hand while she seemed to pull into herself as if she were afraid she might speak again.

~*~

The next Sunday morning, Glory played a familiar song as the pews filled. Attendance had doubled since the first week Eli was there. Of course, Eli was single, very good looking. and semi-famous from the megachurch in Dallas. But the marquee next to the church might be drawing them in. Eli had found the key to the clear doors, and had changed the message to say in big letters, *"Love, Love, Love!"* On the next line in smaller letters he'd spelled out, *"Want it, Need it, Find it, Sunday Morning, 10:00."*

The song ended. She started playing the bridge for

the next song, keeping her voice soft and leaning close to the microphone so she could be heard. "This week, as I thought about God's love for us, I looked at our world and thought how beautiful it is. God could have given us a black and white world. A place where there were no sounds except words. Where there were no flowers and fragrances. Instead, he gave a world with such startling beauty; even the greatest artists can't get it on canvas. He gave us music and children's laughter and birds' songs. And he gave us flowers with scents that can never be copied, and wondrous sea creatures, amazing animals.

"As I thought about all that, I was so overwhelmed with His goodness I couldn't keep from echoing Psalm 18 back to Him, *'I love you, Lord, my strength. The Lord is my rock, my fortress, and my deliverer; my God is my rock, in whom I take refuge, my shield and the horn of my salvation, my stronghold.'* Thank you, Lord." Focused completely on God, she whispered the last three words, and then played the intro for the song.

The worship team started singing, sounding hushed and beautiful, as if God had touched them with the same realization He'd given her.

When the song service was finished, Glory and the rest of the team sat.

Eli stood from his place on the front pew, flipped on his mic, and took the podium. "Musical groups and poets have been speaking of love since time began. Love, sweet love, and only needing love. But God, the ultimate wordsmith, said it even better." Eli flipped open his Bible. "Proverbs 19:22 says, 'What a person desires is unfailing love.' Because love heals. No matter who it is, what they are or what they've been through, love will find a way."

Glory wasn't surprised that their ranks had swollen so quickly. Eli's sermon was beautiful, dynamic, and compelling. And he had a way of focusing on each person in the congregation as if he were talking only to them. Roni must have felt that, too, because, with a glance over her right shoulder, Glory could see her tearing up. Before long, tears were running down her cheeks.

At invitation time, twenty-three people joined the church, and five wanted to be baptized—three women and two men.

While everyone headed for the dressing rooms to prepare, Glory started playing the song they sang after every baptism. Roni, the foster child she'd worried and prayed over for so long, came up to the side of the piano and waited for Glory to finish playing.

Tears crested Roni's lashes. "Miss Glory, I want you to baptize me," she choked out in an emotion-filled whisper.

A thrill shot through Glory. Roni had accepted the Lord! Glory jumped off the bench, accidentally banging several sour notes as she did, to hug the girl as George, the high school boy playing the keyboard, took the melody.

Then the rest of what the girl said filtered in—Roni wanted Glory to baptize her. She nearly sagged against the piano. Instead, she pulled the girl behind a wooden pillar. "Roni, I'm not a minister. I've never baptized anyone."

The girl's face crinkled with puzzlement as a tear spilled onto her cheek and ran to her chin. "Didn't you read us a verse last week that said we're all the same in Jesus?"

Glory thought back to their discussion. Somehow, they'd gotten on the subject of how they were all God's children, no matter who they were, and that race and nationality didn't matter. After all the girls had discussed it a bit, Glory had read from Galatians to them. They'd gone from there to baptism.

Roni really had been listening.

But this girl, this child of God, who'd been through so much, and survived so much, and had every right to be bitter and close-minded, had heard what she'd missed. "You're right, Roni. It said that it doesn't matter who we are because when we're baptized into Christ, we're clothed with Him."

"W-will you baptize me?" How many times had the important people in the girl's life failed her or just ignored her?

But physically baptize her? When a minister of God was present? "We need to pray about this, Roni." They quietly slipped out to an empty room, where they prayed for God's guidance. As they prayed, she could hear the congregation sing a verse of the simple chorus.

She continued to pray, and when the congregation sang the chorus again, she knew. Somehow, she just knew it was right. Her heart slammed hard against her chest wall as she thought about what might happen.

Their church didn't have women as ministers, deacons or elders, much less baptizers she nodded to the girl. "Let's go."

"You'll baptize me?" Roni's face looked open and innocent as she'd never seen it.

Glory's heart was almost too full to answer. She smiled.

They hurried through the hall to the back steps that led to the tiny baptistery dressing rooms. They quickly changed into the garments kept there for baptisms and were waiting as the last person who'd made the confession of faith was immersed.

Eli was watching a person walk out of the water. Having seen baptisms all her life, Glory knew he probably planned to step to the front of the baptistery and have a few closing words with the congregation.

When he saw Roni standing there, his face brightened. "A new sister in Christ?" he asked quietly. When he saw Glory standing next to her, wearing the same clothing, his smile dimmed, and he raised his eyebrows in a silent, "What's going on?"

"Wait here," Glory whispered to Roni. She walked the few paces to Eli. "Roni asked if I could baptize her. She really wants *me* do it. We prayed about it." She held her breath waiting for Eli's reply. She was exposed to the congregation. What would she do if he said no?

He glanced past her to Roni. He smiled, first at Roni, then at her. "I don't see why not," he whispered.

Glory's heart soared. She motioned for Roni to come forward. Roni waded into the warm water. Glory could hear people in the congregation murmuring, but no one said anything she could understand. Eli moved to one side so that he and she flanked the girl. Glory could smell the chlorine as she moved slowly through the water. A little nervous, her voice trembled as she raised it so the whole congregation could hear. "This is Roni Jones. She's Harold and Teresa Knox's foster daughter. Roni has been in my Bible study class for several months now, and we've prayed for her ever since she started coming.

"Just a few moments ago, she asked me to baptize her." She focused on Roni, looking square into her face for any sign that the girl wasn't one hundred percent sincere. "Roni, I have a couple of questions. Do you believe that Jesus is the Christ, the son of the living God? And do you want Him to be your personal savior?"

Roni's face was as radiant as a bride's. "Yes, *oh, yes!*"

"Acts 2:38 says, 'Repent and be baptized every one of you in the name of Jesus Christ for the remission of your sins, and you will receive the gift of the Holy Spirit.' So I baptize you now, Roni Jones, in the name of Jesus. Buried with Christ" —She lay the girl back and under the water and then lifted her— "arise and walk, a new creation in Him."

Roni came up from beneath the water with a smile on her face. "Thank you, Jesus."

Glory's heart was bursting. She forgot that everyone filling the auditorium was waiting. Forgot she should have been speaking so everybody could hear. She put her arm around Roni. "As you reminded me, Galatians three says, 'For all of you who were baptized into Christ have clothed yourselves with Christ. There is neither Jew nor Gentile, neither slave nor free, nor is there male and female, for you are all one in Christ Jesus.' Never forget, Roni, you are clothed in Him."

Roni grabbed her with a splash and hugged her, and before she knew what was happening, Eli was hugging them both.

The church broke into applause and cheers. The cheers might have been from the girls in Glory's Bible study class, but she couldn't be sure.

7

When Sunday school let out the next week, the hallway was more crowded than Eli remembered. He shook hands with several people he thought were new, but with his memory for faces, he couldn't be sure. At least they weren't on the church board. He was sure of that. He was looking for one face in particular. Glory.

When had he started feeling almost lost when she wasn't close by? And how had he not noticed her beauty that day in the snow? Well, the scarf had hidden most of her face, but still. Those eyes...

Brandi ran up out of nowhere and hugged his leg, all memory of their rocky morning apparently forgotten. He knelt beside her. She must have had great fun playing Duck, Duck, Goose or some other action game, because her ponytail dragged to one side of her head and her skirt hung crooked. He gave her a quick hug, surreptitiously straightening her skirt as he did.

Nothing he could do about her hair right now without taking out the barrette and starting over, and she hated it when he used his comb instead of her brush. He didn't want a hissy fit in church.

Brandi grabbed his hand and pointed at Glory

moving toward them.

The smile on Glory's face grew when she spotted them. Was it Brandi who gave it that extra sparkle or was Glory glad to see him? Maybe both? Without thinking, he reached for her hand, but instead of shaking it, he pulled her to him and held it. What was it about touching her that filled him with happiness?

She finally broke their gaze and knelt beside Brandi. "You look as if you had fun in Sunday school this morning. Did you play a game?"

Grinning, Brandi nodded, her ponytail flopping.

Glory quickly snapped the barrette out of the blond strands, rearranged his daughter's tresses and snapped it back in—no whines, tears or tantrums. Was Glory a magician or what?

Roni and Taylor ran up to them. "Hey Brandi, want to go to Kids' Church with us? It's fun."

"And we're having some really good homemade cookies today, so you can spoil your lunch." Roni gave them a brilliant smile, so different from the look she'd given him when he went to their Bible study. "Oh, and Pastor Eli...? You'll remember what we talked about the other day?"

"Don't worry." He nodded. "I won't forget."

Brandi looked up at him as if to ask permission.

"Sure, baby, go with the girls. Have fun."

Brandi hesitated another moment and then ran down the hallway with the bigger girls.

His heart gave a thump.

Glory stepped a little closer, the contact warming him. "She'll be fine."

After six months of worry, doctors, talking to her and for her, waiting for her, working with her and being patient, patient, patient, could she open up and speak to someone else first? He only hoped they'd tell him about it if she did.

After the song service, when he finally got in the pulpit, he noticed every pew had people in it. They weren't all shoulder to shoulder, but some were. And yes, as usual, they were predominantly women, but that was probably true in most churches.

He placed his notes and his Bible on the stand and asked the congregation to rise and pray with him. Funny thing, when he finished praying, he couldn't think about his notes, even though it was a good sermon. Instead, he found himself turning to Matthew 19. He started reading at verse two. "*'He called a little child to Him and placed the child among them. Truly I tell you, unless you change and become like little children, you will never enter the kingdom of heaven.'*"

He slid his notes underneath his Bible. "Did you ever wonder about that verse? If you've ever worked for the Matthews sisters at their daycare, you might have questioned it, or if your child ever had a tantrum in the middle of the store for the entire world to see. I know I doubted it just this morning when Brandi dressed herself for church...in a tank top that was several sizes too small and a net tutu. She got very angry when I told her she couldn't wear it to church.

"But her innocence and her love for that net thing is very real. I saw another group of children, a little older than Brandi, showing their unselfish love for others this week. They came to me and requested that this church *allow* them to use their time and their own money to have a winter carnival in the gym. They want to invite the entire town of Jordan Valley to our campus to get to know us, so people who don't attend can see what being a Christian is all about.

"At a time in their lives when most kids are self-centered and looking for a good time, these girls want to reach out to others. To show them the light of Christ." He talked a little longer as the feeling inside him grew stronger. Finally, he closed his Bible and turned to Glory. "Would you go get Roni and Taylor? I think they should be the ones to take the names of volunteers who are here this morning."

She stared at him for a moment. "They're in Junior Church with all the kids," she answered, a look of doubt on her face.

His stomach roiled as if he'd swallowed an effervescent tablet whole. What would the board think about him cutting the service short? His fizzy belly practically gurgled at the thought, but the other feeling, the one that pulled him to this idea in the first place, grew stronger. "Bring the children to their parents, and have the girls set up with their notebook at that table in the foyer. It's my guess that a lot of our members would like to volunteer to help them."

The members looked a little startled and murmured among themselves.

"Why don't we sing while the girls get ready?" He asked Miss Charlotte where she sat near the organ. "How about a good, old-fashioned revival song?"

Charlotte's smile was sweet as ever as she hustled to the organ and hunted up the music in the hymnal. Soon she was shattering all the eardrums present with the melody. As they started the second verse, the kids from Junior Church ran into the room and found their parents.

When they were finishing the last verse, Glory came in the back doors and nodded. The girls were ready.

The kids had made a signup sheet for people just wanting to volunteer to help out anywhere. They also were jotting down ideas for booths they hadn't thought of.

Halle volunteered to let them have T-shirts at her cost that were imprinted with "Thirsty? Have a sip of Living Water!" John 4: 7-13. On the back it said, "JVC3." They could give away the shirts at the carnival. Retta Tanner, a woman with dark red hair and four grown sons who looked just like her, volunteered to bring her ginormous charcoal grill on wheels and a couple of her four sons to man it. She'd also volunteered to bring in her gentlest horses for the kids to take rides on if it wasn't too cold out.

When most of the people had left the church, Miss Charlotte went to the table where the girls were sitting. "This is such a good idea. I'm so impressed with you girls! But I can think of one more booth we need."

Mrs. Jackson frowned, holding her Bible as she waited near the door. "Well, tell them so we can go. It's time for dinner."

Miss Charlotte nodded, her sweet smile never

wavering. "We need a sign pointing to one of the smaller rooms that says, 'Need Prayer?' We could have a couple of people in there all the time to pray with those who need it."

"Oh, Miss Charlotte, that's a fantastic idea!" Roni bounced in her chair. "And Brother Daniels can be there to pray!"

Dread filled Eli's gut. *Me? I'm not even sure the Lord hears my prayers anymore. Or wants to.* He forced a smile; at least he hoped he did.

Miss Charlotte nodded. "Other people can take turns working in the prayer booth, but I think Brother Eli will want to be there at least part of the time."

Why *doesn't Glory remember this is Roni's thing, not theirs? The girls should make those decisions and be there to pray, not me.* Eli cleared his throat and found his voice. "Since I'm new here, and a relative stranger, maybe you should have members man the prayer booth. I'll drop in from time to time and see if I'm needed." *And I might find a place to hide out.*

Glory didn't speak up. Of course, that could be because her mother and aunt were both talking to her.

Roni and Taylor flipped shut their notebooks. Actually, Roni flipped her notebook, Taylor put away her phone where she'd been making notes. They yelled, "See you this afternoon, Glory!" and dashed out the door.

At last, Glory's aunt and mother nodded hard and hurried out the door with the last of the worshippers, leaving him and Glory alone. She stared at the door with a faraway look and finally, lowered her head as if in prayer. Or was she just stretching tensed neck muscles?

He waited.

After a while, she drew a breath and lifted her hands. "Oh, Father. What a day this has been. Help me to hear Your voice. I need to know if this winter carnival is your will. If it is, please bless it and our town. If it isn't, please stop us now."

He understood. This woman spoke directly with God, almost like Moses, and not surprisingly, expected Him to answer.

~*~

When the day of the carnival arrived, Eli dressed Brandi in her T-shirt. The shirt had a pitcher and most of the words printed in black, but Living Water in brilliant silver sparkly letters. Since it was too big, he put another shirt under it and let her wear her favorite leggings with rainbow colors swirling over them. She wore shoes that lit up as she walked.

When they got to the church, Star glanced up with a big smile from a section right in the middle of the gym floor, edged with hay bales. She finished pouring something from a bucket that looked like sand, set it down and climbed over the hay to hurry to him. "Can Brandi help me in the Smallers' section today? It's for kids under five only."

His daughter was so excited, she was standing on tiptoe and trembling all over. "How about it, Brandi. Want to be Star's assistant for the night?"

Brandi nodded so hard, he was afraid the pigtails he'd labored over to get even would fall out. She grabbed Star's hand and glued herself to the woman's leg.

"I hadn't heard about that section."

"Are you kidding? Mom and Aunt Rosemary discussed it with Glory until she agreed, as long as Beany and Sam sponsored it. We have bouncy ponies, treasure hunts in dried corn instead of sand, a fishing booth and this funny little bounce house that looks like a slide—all kiddo scaled."

"Does that mean we grownups can't try out the slide, just to be sure it's safe?" He put on a mock frown before smiling at her.

"We might have to, for safety sake."

They laughed.

Glory called all the workers together. "We've been praying about tonight for some time now. How about we all pray together before our guests show up?"

The handsome woman with dark red hair and two red-headed sons—Tanner?—who were just outside working at their big charcoal grill on wheels, heard through the open doors, and came in to join the group. Mrs. Jackson and Miss Charlotte were stirring up fruit drink in five-gallon water dispensers, but stopped to move into the group with the rest.

Glory looked across the room at him and opened her mouth to ask him to pray—after all, preachers were normally designated prayers—as Halle rushed through the door, a box heaping over with T-shirts in her arms. "Sorry I'm late. I just finished these shirts. There'll be plenty to give away, but I need help carrying in the rest."

"First, we're praying," Glory answered, a smile in her eyes.

"Then I'm just in time!" With a huge grin, the blonde dropped the cardboard box and stepped into the circle. She took the hands of the teens she stood between. The boy on her left gazed at her, his mouth open and his face turning red as he stared. The girl on Halle's right rolled her eyes and shook her head.

"Eli?" Glory called from the other side of their haphazard circle as the rest of the group joined hands. "Will you pray?"

Yep, designated pray-er. And he was probably the last one they should ask. "Of course," he answered, shifting into Minister Mode. "Father God, creator of all things, we thank You..." He pontificated. Inside, he shrank because he knew he spoke only to the rafters. Why couldn't he pray like Glory? Why couldn't he speak from his heart the way Miranda had? What was wrong with him? He stopped talking mid-sentence, maybe mid-word. He wasn't really sure.

If the others wanted to walk away and get busy again, they could.

But for once, this time at least, he intended to pray from his heart. *Forgive my self-centeredness, Father. Please help me to speak to only you without pride or sin in my heart.* "Lord," he finally continued, his voice breaking and barely above a whisper, "we know that all good things come from you. Everyone who comes to our carnival is your child. Give us eyes to see those who are hurting, Lord. Keep us from being so busy that we can't see those in need. Amen."

The kids beside him let go of his hands

Eli realized his face was wet. And not only *his* face.

More than a few people in the circle were wiping their eyes.

"I'll be right back." Eli noticed the first booth just inside the gym doors was the memory verse booth. The girls had posted verses on the walls and were busy lining up the wide rubber bands on a stand that they would jot the scripture the guests learned and the first few words.

Games were being set up around the gym. A basketball hoop was wrapped with crepe paper in what he assumed was the town's school colors—red and white. A little farther down, clear plastic cups were being filled with water, and a tiny goldfish slipped into each one. Someone else had just spilled a bag of brightly colored ping pong balls, and they were scrambling to catch them. Near the corner of the gym, someone was pinning small, colorful balloons to a board. Funny, they didn't ask their blowhard preacher to help inflate them.

Eli went out the door nearest the church and hurried to the back door. Unlocking the building, he rushed to his office, found a small Bible and a little notebook, and slipped them into the back pockets of his jeans. As he started back down the hall, he passed the prayer room. The time was drawing near when people would start arriving, but something or Someone pulled him inside as if he had no choice.

Shadows filled the room, but a couch and a couple of chairs were in place. Urgency filled him, or was it dread? Taking a deep breath, he sat. He skipped his usual silent opening phrase—"Get me out of this small town"—and went to the heart of the matter. "Oh, Lord, I need you. Please, reach into my heart, remove anything that can keep me from You. And if I touch someone today, let them see only You."

He slipped from the chair to his knees on the floor. "I love You, Lord, my strength. The Lord is my rock, my fortress and my deliverer, my God is my rock in whom I take refuge, my shield and the horn of my salvation, my stronghold. I called to the Lord, who is worthy of praise...To the faithful You show Yourself faithful, to the blameless You show Yourself blameless, to the pure You show Yourself pure, but to the devious, You show Yourself shrewd. You save the humble but bring low those whose eyes are haughty. Make me faithful, Lord. Make me blameless and pure and most important, teach me humility. And, Father, please keep my lamp burning. Only You, Lord, can turn my darkness into light."

He drew a cleansing breath, struggled to his feet, dried his face with a tissue from the box someone— Glory?—kept there. After straightening his jeans, he brushed the wrinkles out of his T-shirt.

When he stepped back outside, the entire church property looked as though it had changed somehow. The people looked brighter, more interesting, as if each was a person he couldn't wait to get to know. Maybe things outside him hadn't changed. No, he was pretty sure it was his insides that had. Locking the church door, he smelled the grill going strong.

If that didn't get the neighborhood's attention, what would?

The clatter of horses' hooves stopped him as a miniature stagecoach pulled by a pair of matching horses came down the alleyway between the church and gym. Two more of Mrs. Tanner's red-haired sons were in the driver's seat.

"Howdy, Preach!" one of the Tanners shouted with a nod.

Was it just a few days ago that Halle calling him "Preach" had offended him? Funny, now it seemed a pleasant nickname. "Howdy!" Eli shouted back. "Is that a real stagecoach you're driving?"

The second twin gave him a half grin. "Naw. It's a shell that fits over our farm wagon. It's about half size. Want to take a ride?"

Almost magically, Eli was surrounded by Brandi and the other children, all hoping for a ride. Since the kids belonged to members who were working to get the carnival ready to begin, he nodded.

As he helped them into the coach, a clown cavorted toward them in a bouncing run. She wore overalls cut off just above the knee over ratty red long-johns that had faded to a dull pink, and floppy, green high-tops—probably the reason she ran like a car with lopsided wheels. And on her head sat a battered straw hat with a giant purple flower pinned to the front. The woman wore full clown make up with freckles and a giant red grin. "Me, too! Me, too!" she squealed, exposing two gigantic front teeth as she bounced up and down.

Recognition hit him with a pang. "Glory?"

The beautiful woman who prayed as if she were in God's very presence, and played the piano as if she'd been given extra fingers, dressed *and acting* like a circus clown?

He wouldn't have been more surprised if one of the horses pulling the stagecoach started singing opera—and not nearly as entertained.

She stopped with one foot inside the coach. "Not tonight," she answered, her own lips, painted white, curved her mouth almost as large as the fake clown grin. "Tonight, I'm Esmerelda Clown."

"Well, Ms. Merelda, let's get a move on!" With his shoulder to her rear-end, he pretended to shove as hard as he could while she grunted and carried on as if she were about to fall to the ground.

When they were finally settled inside, with the kids all piled on top of each other and on them, the coach started rolling.

Funny, he'd never realized how rough a stagecoach ride would have been. But the kids loved it, especially with Glory sliding out of her seat to the floor as if her bones were made of pancake batter, then bouncing up to hit her head on the roof.

The children laughed hard at her antics.

He didn't try to hide his grin. "Do you know where laughter comes from?" he asked.

"Cartoons!" one child shouted.

"Clowns!"

"Our stomachs!"

He shook his head as he looked from face to face. Finally, he focused on Brandi. "Laughter comes from God! He loves us soooooo much, he wants us to be happy. If you watch, you can find something funny just about everywhere you go. But you have to look for it because sometimes He hides it."

"Like a treasure?" one of the Mills kids asked in a high voice.

"Exactly. Happiness is a treasure, straight from God. OK, each one of you, tell me one thing that makes you happy." He stopped, his gaze on Glory. "You first, Ms. Merelda."

She shook her head so hard, her hat flew off. "You first."

He held her gaze, something burning inside him. "Something that makes me happy?" He held her gaze, hoping she could read *you make me happy* in his mind. Finally, he answered, "What makes me happy is clowns."

The kids cheered as if he'd just made a winning touchdown in the last second on the clock.

Glory's eyes widened as she bobbed her head in a fake struggle to swallow. Clearing her throat, she finally tore her gaze from his. "Gol-ly."

He forced his focus away from her. "How about you, Zoey? What makes you happy?"

"Cake!" the girl answered.

They went around the stagecoach and everyone answered, except Brandi, of course. The stagecoach pulled back into the alleyway and Eli asked. "OK, your turn now. What makes a clown happy, Ms. Merelda?"

Even though the false teeth obscured most of her bottom lip, her mouth trembled. She took a long, audible breath, glanced around at the children and leaned forward as if she were going to tell them a secret. "What makes me happy is….short Sunday sermons!"

The children went wild with laughter, rocking in their seats and kicking their feet off the floor.

One of the drivers opened the door. "Jordan Valley Station. Ever'body out!"

The children thanked the Tanner brothers for their ride and ran inside.

The gym had started filling with people. A line of kids waited nearby, controlled by Mrs. Jackson. "All right, boys and girls, come and get in the stagecoach. Stay away from those horses now, because they wear steel shoes. The shoes are to protect their hooves, but they'd put a big knot on your noggin if they kicked you. Did you know that stagecoaches like this one was how most people traveled here in Oklahoma before we had cars?" The woman was a natural teacher.

Eli stepped back into the carnival.

One of the teens running the basketball toss called him over. "Want to take a chance, Brother Eli?"

"Sure." He reached for a ball.

The broad-shouldered young man put his hand atop it, keeping it in place. "Three shots for a memory verse. Do you know one?" The boy lifted one eyebrow, a smile quirking his mouth.

"Does it have to be one of the ones posted or will

any verse do?" Eli asked him.

The youth shrugged one shoulder. "Suit yourself."

"'The Lord provided a huge fish to swallow Jonah. And Jonah was in the belly of the fish three days and three nights.' Jonah 1:17."

With a grin, the young man moved his hand.

"Now I have a question for you." Eli shot the ball toward the hoop. And missed.

The kid handed him another ball. "What is it?"

Eli aimed at the hoop again, this time more carefully. "Why the red and white and gold crepe paper? Are those Jordan Valley's school colors?"

"Nope."

The surprise caused Eli's second shot to bounce off the rim. It had to be the surprise. He was a better shot than that. At least, he used to be.

The boy handed him his third ball. "They're a silent sermon. Washed in the blood, whiter than snow. And a gold crown of life."

This time Eli's shot swished through the net.

The girl working in the booth with the young man took one of the cheap, brightly colored plastic bead necklaces and hung it around his neck. "Way to go, Brother Eli. If you can make it, then anyone should be able to. I mean since you're a preacher and old and all. Right?"

The boy elbowed the girl. "Don't say stuff like that, even if it's true. It's kinda rude."

"Oh!" The girl giggled before singing out, "Sor-ry."

Chuckling, Eli headed toward the Need Prayer

booth. Brandi ran up to him, grabbed him around the leg. When she looked up, she had a cat's face painted on hers, complete with a pair of whiskers glued on. She meowed, and the breath froze in his lungs.

Brandi spoke. Well, sort of.

For the first time in over six months, Brandi had voluntarily made a noise. Not really a word, but a sound was progress, wasn't it?

"Where did you get that kitty face, beautiful?" he asked, praying she would answer.

Instead of answering, she tugged his hand over to where Halle was painting the face of a clown on another little girl. She gave her a sparkle mole on the side of her face and helped her out of the tall chair. The little girl giggled as she hopped down and ran off with Brandi.

"You're next, Brother Eli."

Thinking only of Brandi and her meow, Eli sat in the chair.

Halle tucked a paper napkin into the collar of his T-shirt. "What kind of face do you want?"

He glanced toward the Smallers' section where Brandi started digging in a plastic pool filled with corn. The sound of her sweet voice saying meow resounded in his mind. "A cat."

Halle chuckled and tossed her braid behind her shoulder. "Cats are for sweet little girls. We'll make you a tiger."

"Close enough." He tore his gaze from his daughter to glance at the woman who'd turned to her basket full of paints. "But let's leave off the whiskers."

She nodded and turned back toward him with a jar of something in her hand. "Do you have a memory verse for me?"

He nodded. "When Aaron and all the Israelites saw Moses, his face was radiant, and they were afraid to come near him. Exodus 34:30."

~*~

Glory glanced around the gym for Eli. She needed him to head for the prayer room. There were women already in there, waiting for him to pray with them. She started around the big room, looking into games and places where he could be. As she started past the Berean Class's table where they were serving the hotdogs and nachos, she saw old Mrs. Lewis preparing a disposable boat of chips and cheese.

"Hello, Mrs. Lewis. How are you?"

"I told you that you could call me Margaret now. I haven't worked in the old doctor's office in many years, and you're all grown up." Glory had never seen the woman without the sweet smile she was wearing.

"Now don't wear yourself out. You haven't been out of the hospital very long."

"Oh, that silly Dr. Halstead just put me in the hospital because he couldn't keep his kids from running into the shop and coming to my house and bothering me all day. As if his children could be a bother." She chuckled a warm laugh. "You know, the oldest one helps me when I get yarn shipments, and to pay her, I'm teaching his girls to knit."

Glory thought about the now single doctor with all his children. "How many kids does he have now?"

"Five. They keep him busier than his practice, I think." Mrs. Lewis leaned closer and lowered her voice to a loud whisper. "You know, he needs a good wife this time, Glory. One that won't run off and leave him with her kids as well as the ones they make together. With that daycare, you'd be perfect for him. And you aren't getting any young—"

"Oh, no! Not me, Mrs. Lewis." Glory held back the shriek that rose in her throat. "I have all the kids I can handle now."

The woman wrinkled her forehead as if she didn't know what Glory was talking about.

"I mean the daycare kids. I couldn't handle dealing with other people's kids all day and then go home to a house full of someone else's kids at night." Glory glanced at her watch. "Oops, I better run. Bye."

As Glory scurried away from Mrs. Lewis's matchmaking attempt, the woman said something in her soft, high voice. It might have been goodbye, but it also might have been good try. Glory didn't wait to find out.

When Glory finally made it to the prayer room a few moments later, the place was crowded. There were mostly women in the room, but a few men milled around, too. Eli stood behind a lectern writing in a small notebook while Roni sat at a nearby table keeping track of the prayer requests on lined paper.

Holding her hat on her head, Glory wound her way through the crowd to stand by until Eli finished listening to the woman in front of him. When she finally finished talking, Eli tore a piece of paper from his notebook and handed it to the woman, who *accidentally* grabbed his hand along with the paper. "I've listed a few verses here for you to pray. They aren't magic, but it is God's word. I think it'll help you." He stepped from behind the stand and put his hand on the woman's shoulder. As he prayed, the woman pushed her glasses up on her nose, shoved her light brown hair behind one ear, stepped in and wrapped her arm around his waist, causing Glory's stomach to tense.

Maybe having Eli in the prayer room wasn't such a good idea after all.

When they finished praying, Eli dropped his hand from her shoulder and tried to step away, but the woman held tight. He glanced around as if looking for someone to help him get free. Maybe Glory should call Halle and borrow a pry bar.

He sent her a pointed and desperate *help me!* look and as his eyebrows rose higher and higher. With a shake of her head, she stepped in and turned her clown grin on high. "The minister has to pray with others now. Thank you for being with us."

The woman frowned and lifted one side of her mouth. For a moment, Glory thought she might snarl, but she finally released Eli. "If I remember something else I need you to pray for, can I come back?" She gazed at Eli with a hopeful look.

One prayer to a customer, Glory was tempted to answer, but instead, put her hands on the woman's shoulders and turned her toward the door. "God hears all His children. You can pray to Him yourself. You don't have to have someone else do it for you."

When they reached the exit, the woman started out the door but turned back to get one last look at Eli. "But that man is so pretty, and that voice! I enjoy it a bunch more when he prays." With a wink, she turned and wandered into the crowd.

Glory hurried back to Eli's side, where he was once more writing in his little notebook. "Excuse me," she said to the blonde talking to him.

"Hey, it's *my* turn," the woman snapped.

Glory nodded, then led Eli a few steps from the stand. "You probably need to keep that podium between you and them," she whispered.

He glanced at the blonde, who now was holding on to the stand with both hands as if she were ready to leap right over it. "You're gonna need a bigger podium."

She chuckled softly and shook her head. "I'll move through the group and see if I can shorten the line."

He gave her a half smile. "Good luck with that. Roni already tried to get them to make two lines, but it seems everyone wants the H-P-I-C to pray with them."

"What's H-P-I-C?"

He chuckled a self-deprecating laugh and turned so he faced away from the crowd. "H-P-I-C—Head Preacher in Charge. For some reason, people think we're the best pray-ers."

She tried not to laugh out loud.

The blonde had folded her arms in a pout.

Eli turned his back to the room, shielding her completely, slid his fingers to the back of Glory's neck and stole the breath right out of her lungs. "You look like a tired clown."

"I am tired, and we're just getting started." Had he stepped closer to her or did it just feel like it?

"Tell you what." His voice grew softer, more intimate as he used the tips of his fingers to ease some of the tension from her neck. Her nape started to tingle. "When this carnival is finished, I'll meet you here. We'll spend some quality time together."

Finally, she remembered to breathe. "Cleaning up?"

"Yep." He moved the light massage from her neck down her arm, spreading the shivery feeling even farther. His gaze burned through her. "Or we could let the classes do the cleanup tomorrow instead of having a lesson."

She tried to ignore the quivery feeling, but it was next to impossible. Her spine might be melting. She gasped for a breath and tried to remember what she'd been saying. Oh, yeah. "Little kids are out here. They can't." Did that make sense? She wasn't sure and wouldn't be if she didn't step away from him. She'd probably melt into a puddle at his feet.

With a Herculean effort, she pulled away from his touch and glanced past him at the blonde who'd started tapping her foot. A long breath cleared Glory's mind a little. She lifted her hat and plopped it on the back of her head, making the big flower flop. Maybe next time, she'd get a flower with a squirt attachment.

"You know, you might be able to get these friends to help."

8

The next morning, Glory played the introduction to the first song, putting as much bounce into it as she could muster. She'd been amazed at the number of people who'd stayed to clean up after the carnival, especially the Tanner family with all those boys. They'd stayed and so had their friends, which made clean up much easier than she'd expected.

She'd even had trouble getting the Berean class to go home until finally, Mrs. Jackson declared that old ladies needed their rest and they were all leaving. Apparently, they knew better than to argue with her.

But even with all the help, it had been late when Grace got to bed. She'd have given a dollar to stay in bed a little longer, but she had a responsibility, and Mom and Aunt Rosemary wouldn't let her forget.

She pushed the rhythm a little faster. The worship team quickly caught up with her. Someone started clapping, and the congregation joined in.

As they sang, the church filled. Ushers asked people to move toward the middle of the row so others could slide in beside them. Soon, they were setting up chairs along the back of the sanctuary, and as quickly as they put one in place, someone came to sit in it.

By the time the song service was over, every available space in the room was filled, even the front row, which was normally reserved for people making decisions. For a moment, she was afraid they'd bring someone to sit beside her on the piano stool.

Well, it couldn't be helped. The team could sit in the chairs at the edge of the stage, where they normally sat during communion or if someone sang a solo. By decision time, the worship team would be back on the stage, anyway. Still, it felt strange to sit there.

Eli went to the podium and raised both hands in welcome and waited for silence. He spoke quietly. "'I pray that out of His glorious riches He may strengthen you with power through His Spirit in your inner being, so that Christ may dwell in your hearts through faith. And I pray that you, being rooted and established in love, may have power, together with all the Lord's holy people, to grasp how wide and long and high and deep is the love of Christ, and know this love that surpasses knowledge—that you may be filled to the measure of all the fullness of God.'" He quoted the scripture as if the words were original with him. He whispered parts and got strong in places, and when he quoted the last words—*filled to the measure of all the fullness of God*—he sounded as if he were close to tears.

He took a long breath and blew it out. "'Now to Him Who is able to do immeasurably more than all we ask or imagine, according to His power that is at work within us, to Him be glory in the church and in Christ Jesus throughout all generations, forever and ever!'" He started in a broken tone, but by the time he finished, he was nearly shouting. "Those are Paul's words to the Ephesians. Ephesus was the fourth greatest city in the world, and filled with wizards, sorcerers, witches, astrologers, diviners, and palm readers. But after they received God's word, magicians publicly burned their books, which were worth fifty thousand pieces of silver, each.

"That was a great victory over falsehood and demonism. You might think we don't have that sort of thing these days. Witches may not sit around stirring their caldrons."

One of the girls walked across the stage behind him, dressed like a Halloween witch, complete with broom.

"But there are those who practice witchcraft. We don't have wizards with pointy hats."

Another young person walked onto the stage, dressed in a robe, star-covered conical hat, and carrying a wand.

"But there are those who read their horoscope every day, wear their zodiac sign as a necklace or bracelet. How many of you have gone to a carnival and had your fortune told—'just for fun'?" Now the wizard helped a girl in a fortuneteller's costume carry out a small table. They tossed a cloth over it, pulled a chair up to it and place a crystal ball on it that looked suspiciously like an inverted goldfish bowl. The fortuneteller pulled up a chair and waved her hands over the ball.

"Who among us wouldn't give a lot of money for a crystal ball, if it really worked? According to the

Bible, that's of the devil. Ever wonder why? Because God is the only Person who is omniscient, omnipresent and omnipotent. Only God knows all, can be all places at all times and do all things, and so He doesn't want us depending on anyone but Him. When we get up in the morning, He wants us to look to Him, not a horoscope. When we are in doubt, He wants us to trust Him, not a talisman or lucky coin. When we need to know something, God wants us to ask Him, not look at a piece of glass or a charlatan.

"We need to be 'rooted and established in love and have power to grasp how wide and long and high and deep is the love of Christ.' His love is more than we can understand with our feeble human minds. He loves us and wants all good things for us. You know, God never tells us no unless He has an even better yes for us.

"God isn't some far off being, watching to see what we'll do each day. He's involved with our every thought and deed. He sees when even a sparrow falls and knows how many hairs you have on your head. Of course, for some of us, like Harold Knox, that's not saying much." Eli gestured toward the man, whose head was nearly bald.

Harold guffawed as the audience tittered.

"But someone like his daughter, Roni, who has enough hair to supply three people, for God to have the hairs on her head numbered is a big deal." He glanced over his shoulder at the "witch" and winked.

"But unless you know the depth and breadth and length of His love, you'll never understand." He turned to the living illustrations behind him again. "Thank you for your help, kids."

The kids gathered up their things and left the stage.

"God is the one true thing in this world. Not magic, or luck, or anything else. And the only way to God is through Jesus, His Son."

Glory started softly playing the invitation song. Blinking as if waking from a dream, the worship team moved into place and started singing.

People streamed to the front of the auditorium. The elders and deacons moved into place to pray with those who needed prayer and talk to the others. Women made the majority of the decisions, but a few had men with them. A few men came by themselves.

Sixteen people made the decision to be baptized, and nineteen more placed their membership with JVC3. Seven members, most of whom Glory either didn't know or hadn't seen in years, rededicated their lives.

When the service finally ended, Glory gathered her things and headed for the door. As she entered the foyer, Mark Chambers, the Sunday school superintendent, and most of the board hovered there.

With nearly everyone except the staff gone, Harold Knox looked at the others. "If this keeps up, we'll have to either go to two services or build on so we'll have room."

"Not that it's about numbers, but how many did we have today?" Eli asked.

"It was record-setting," Mark Chambers

answered, rocking onto his toes and back to his heels. "More than even our biggest Easter service in the past. I'm wondering if we need to find some property and build an entirely new church."

Unable to keep from rolling her eyes, Glory walked out the front door. No telling how long they would discuss building. By the time they came together again, they'd probably be talking about hiring an architect. But they shouldn't, because the numbers were there to see and hear Eli. And she knew without a doubt, he wouldn't be staying long.

~*~

Monday morning, Brandi came into the daycare and grabbed Glory around the leg.

"Morning, Brandi!" Glory glanced around to see if Eli had come in as he usually did. "Where's your dad?"

Brandi looked at her with big eyes, but no answer.

A few minutes later, the Mills kids came stampeding in.

"Can we play with your puppies? Please? Can I have Princess Perky?" Sophie asked, bouncing on her toes.

"No, me!" Zoey out shouted her. "Me first! I want Princess Popie."

Brandi's bottom lip poked out, but she didn't say anything.

Glory went to the cabinet where she'd stored the puppets and brought out three of them. Princess Precious was the last one. When the royal princess made her appearance, the Mills girls started jumping up and down and fake crying for her. "Me! Me! I want her first!"

Glory held the doll upright. "I'll tell you what. I'll let the first one who can say her name properly play with her first.

By now, the Mills girls were gyrating, jumping and being wild.

"Now, listen. Her name," Glory said with all the drama she could muster, "is Princess Precious. Can you remember that?"

"I can! I can!" Zoey shrieked. "Pinces Pukey."

Glory shook her head. "Want to try it, Sophie?"

The little girl nodded hard. "Princess Popeye."

"Not quite." Glory looked at Brandi. She'd speak when she was ready. "I guess I'll put the Princess away until someone can say her name."

Brandi reached up and took the puppet by the hand. "Princess Precious," she murmured in the softest voice audible to the human ear.

A thrill of joy threaded through Glory's entire body. She tried to hide her excitement at Brandi's words. *She's speaking!* She wanted to scream, grab someone else to hear her. *Brandi said two words in a row!* Instead, she held tight until she could speak without screeching. "Right!" *So much for not screeching.* She softened her voice. "Her name is Princess Precious."

Glory fitted the puppet on Brandi's small hand, then seeing the other two girls preparing to melt down or cry hysterically, she went to the emergency supply drawer and pulled it open. After sorting a moment, she pulled out two more tiaras, one for Zoey's puppet and one for Sophie's. "Here we go. Now we're all serving royalty."

Zoey curled one side of her mouth and looked with contempt at Glory from beneath lowered eyebrows. "OK. But it's my turn to play with Princess Pinker next."

Sophie whipped her head around to look at Zoey. "Nu-huh. I get to—"

"If it causes a fuss, when Brandi's turn is over, I'll put Princess Precious back in the storage closet, and she'll stay there. No one will get to play with her."

Zoey blinked and, almost magically, her entire face transformed. "It's OK. Sophie can have the next turn. I'll wait for mine."

Oh, yeah. Zoey needed a T-shirt that said in big, sparkly letters, *Been there, done that*. Play the game, give in, let sister or brother go first, and have a better chance of getting what she really wanted.

Rather than play into her strategy, Glory nodded. "Thank you, Zoey! That's kind of you."

Zoey cocked her head as if waiting for Glory to give her next dibs. The sweet smile she'd pasted on her face slowly melted. "Princesses are stupid, anyway. They're for babies."

Brandi stared at the girl for a moment as if judging her words, then with a shrug turned her back on Zoey and made Princess Precious act as if she were talking to Sophie.

Together the girls went into the playhouse—an area with a play kitchen and child-sized furniture, where they knelt behind the kids' table and pretended to have a puppet show—without words, of course.

Zoey watched them go, muttered, "Stupid," dropped the non-princess puppet and her crown on the floor and walked away.

"Miss Zoey, you pick that up," Star said from across the room. "We put away our toys here."

"Well, they aren't being nice to me. I wanted to play, and they left me out!" Zoey's words were hot.

Star, middle child and the one who always imagined herself left out, jerked her gaze to Sophie and Brandi. "Girls! We do *not* leave anyone out."

"Miss Star?" Glory said her sister's name as if it was a question. "Could I talk to you a moment?"

Star changed her focus to Glory and then shifted back to the girls. "Those girls—"

"Please?" Glory interrupted before she could say more. "Let it go. We'll talk about it later."

After a long glare, Star went back to the game she was playing with the boys.

Glory looked into Zoey's face. "Why don't you all play together?"

Zoey raised an eyebrow. "Is it my turn to be Princess Poppy yet?"

"Not yet. Brandi isn't through with her turn."

The girls played with the puppets in the playhouse, with the princess serving tea to the others. Sophie had her turn with the puppet. Glory had set a timer in the hope of making everything fair. After lunch, the kids all lay down for thirty minutes. Sophie wanted the princess for a nap partner, but Glory said toys needed to be put away. After naps, Zoey grabbed for the princess, but Sophie's turn wasn't over according to the timer. Before the timer dinged, Janyce came to pick up her kids. Zoey, Sophie, and Liam put away their toys and got the things they'd brought with them.

Eli came in to pick up Brandi.

Both Eli and Janyce were there much earlier than usual.

"Slow day at the church?" Glory teased.

"Funny how not a lot happens there on Monday, but by the time the weekend gets here, we're much busier."

Zoey's bottom lip was poked out because her turn with the princess had to wait until Tuesday. As she slid her arm into her jacket sleeve, she said, "Brandi *talkedted.*"

Glory frowned at Zoey.

Brandi had spoken. Twice.

And Glory hadn't told Eli about it. If he found out from someone else, he'd probably be upset. *Mea Culpa.*

He gave Zoey an adult smile and nodded, which usually meant, *Hey, I'm a grown up, and I don't get kid talk.* Hopefully, it meant that this time, too.

His smile grew vague until his gaze found Star; then it brightened. "Star, can I talk to you a minute?"

Star? Eli wanted to talk to Star? Glory swallowed past the car-sized lump in her throat and tried to breathe. OK, maybe he hadn't liked the kisses they'd shared. Or maybe he was the kind of guy who liked variety and had never lived in a small town where dating sisters at the same time was against the rules. She'd known guys who got the stuffing beat out of them for doing that, and not always by the sisters they were dating. Sometimes the sisters' friends did it for them. Besides, she'd thought *they'd* had something. Turning, Glory started picking up the blocks Star had been playing with the boys. This time it didn't bother her to smash the intricate structure Star had been working on.

A glance at Star and Eli told her nothing, except that they were very comfortable with each other. He was leaning against the wall, grinning, with his hands in his pockets while Star tossed back her head and laughed.

When Glory had the blocks all picked up, she took the storage box and slammed it onto the shelf where it belonged. After picking up several of the toys that popped out, she tossed them back and headed for the puppets. She picked up all three and stormed to the storeroom, anger warring with guilt. The dolls were causing nothing but trouble with the girls, and even though Brandi had spoken when they were out, she hadn't said much. It wasn't as if there'd been a real breakthrough.

Glory's heart thumped. Maybe she should tell Eli about it, anyway. The air thickened, making it hard to breathe as her conscience bit hard. She started back to the playroom. Even if he were throwing her over for her baby sister, she still needed to tell him about Brandi speaking. It was the right and mature thing to do.

Eli walked in.

She glanced up. A pang jolted through her stomach as his gaze burned into her. Almost the same way as the other night, he backed her into the room until she could go no farther.

"We're going out to dinner tonight—"

"Who? You and Star?" She lifted her chin and hoped he could see a challenge in her eyes. At least she tried to put one there.

He put one hand on the wall, next to her head. "Of course I'm not going with Star. You and I are going into Tulsa for dinner and a show tonight. Just the two of us. Star is babysitting Brandi."

"She is?"

He put the other hand on the other side of her head. Now he had her surrounded, but for some reason, she didn't mind. With her heart going crazy and tingles careening throughout her body and places warming that, well, probably shouldn't be heating up, how could she?

Almost as if he were doing pushups, he leaned in and kissed her.

Her knees melted and those places that had been heating morphed into molten lava.

"So put on something that doesn't say, 'Hi, there. I work in a daycare'. Harold Knox and his wife have given me their tickets to the Performance Center, and I want to take you. We leave in thirty minutes." With another heated kiss, he pushed away.

She prayed she wouldn't just slide down the wall.

"I'll be back soon." He turned to leave. After

taking three steps, he looked at her again, and just his gaze made her feel beautiful. Desirable. Wanted. "Make that twenty minutes. Or fifteen, even. And it really doesn't matter what you wear."

When she could feel her extremities again, she pulled out her phone. "Halle? I'm going on a date, and *I need help!*"

"I'm on my way," Halle answered without a question, bless her heart.

Glory headed for her bedroom. What did she have that didn't say, 'Hi, there. I work in a daycare?' Her red sweater with the lace collar had a Scotty dog on it— very daycare-esque. T-shirts with cartoon characters? No. Rainbow covered scrubs? No, way.

Halle walked in, her blonde hair pulled back. "How's it going?"

"Not good. Eli invited me to go to the PC in Tulsa with him tonight, and his only request was that I can't wear anything that looks like a daycare worker." Tension filling her, she pointed at her clothing strewn bed. "Everything I own says daycare. I might as well wear a neon sign around my neck."

"We'll find something." Halle went to Glory's dresser and rifled until she found a knot of scarves. "Maybe we can use something in here to camouflage the babysitter look."

They covered her bed with nearly every shirt in her closet until Halle, deep inside, let out a yelp. "Found it!" Halle emerged, looking a little frazzled but carrying her pink sweater set with tiny glass beads that made it sparkle.

"I forgot all about that. I hope it still fits."

Halle nodded confidently. "It'll fit. And Eli will love it."

Glory jumped into the shower while Halle filtered through her jewelry box, looking for something to complement the sweaters.

Glory, wrapped in a big towel, threw on some makeup while Halle held up the jewelry she'd found. "Want to wear this diamond dewdrop?"

Glory glanced her way. "I don't think so."

"Then how about this cameo necklace?" She held up the cameo that had been Glory's grandmother's. "It looks as if it could be an antique."

"Perfect. And I'll feel like I have Grandmother with me." She dressed in the sweaters and a pair of jeans with a line of small rhinestones down the side.

Halle fastened on the necklace and Glory picked up her brush.

Before she could decide what to do with her hair—wear it up or down—someone knocked on the door to their living quarters. Repeatedly.

"That's Eli." Glory yanked the brush hard. "It hasn't been fifteen minutes, yet. Maybe ten. Twelve at the most. "Halle, will you go to the door? Tell him I'll be ready in just a moment."

"You bet." Halle set down a pair of boots she'd found in the closet and left to answer the door.

Why was Eli there already? Did he think she was a quick-change artist? Or had a closet full of ready-to-date-wear? She snorted as she slipped on high heel boots and zipped them up the side. *Ouch*. It'd had been a while since she'd worn anything except her beloved running shoes, in which she'd never actually run a step. Heels weren't made for walking. Not very far, anyway.

She glanced in the mirror. Her eyes looked too big for her face, and her hair was starting to frizz. At least, they would be outside Jordan Valley. And, hopefully, she'd have fun and stop thinking about other people's children for a while.

~*~

Eli waited at the door for someone to let him in. He'd been there, knocking until his knuckles smarted. Was Glory hiding out? Had she decided she didn't want to go out with him? He wasn't late, was he? He'd said twenty minutes, and it had been at least a good— he glanced at his phone—ten. *Oops.*

"Hello, Preach!" Halle opened the family's door. "How's it shaking?"

"Fine. Fine." Why was she answering the Matthewses door? "Uh, Glory here?"

"Oh, yeah. She's getting ready. Want to sit down?"

"No. If she's ready, we'd better get going. We're going to the PC."

"I know. She told me."

"How did you get in?" he asked before setting foot inside.

She tossed her head, her braid switched around. "Through the back. That door is nearly always unlocked, and if it's not, a credit card will open it."

He thought about that for a moment, his stomach tensing. "Does everyone in town know about their easy to open back door?"

"Naw. Just the kids in school who helped Glory and Star sneak in a time or two. Or twenty."

He didn't know whether to laugh or keep his mouth shut and just nod. He kept quiet while Halle went back to where he assumed Glory's room was. His professors had warned him about small towns and the people in them who liked playing pranks. He wasn't sure if this was one or not. If it wasn't, and the Matthews house had a break in some time, the criminal might clean them out, find the parsonage key, and make his way there.

Where his baby, Brandi, slept. His everything. Not that he'd like it if anyone's house was broken into, but he'd rip the hide off anyone who tried anything with his daughter. And then he'd tell God the guy died. That would be as much as the guy deserved.

The more he thought about the Matthewses leaving a door unlocked, the tenser his stomach grew. He needed to talk to Glory about that, maybe offer to fix it, for her good as much as for his. He glanced at the time on his phone. It had been twenty minutes at least now. Where was Glory? What could take—

He heard her heels clicking on the tile floor before he saw her. And when he saw her, everything else disappeared. No wonder they'd named her Glory; she looked glorious. Hair falling around her shoulders. And her top—pinkish but soft looking—complemented her flawless complexion. "Hello," he whispered. Where had his voice gone? Maybe he should start breathing and try that again. He cleared his throat and took a deep, lung expanding breath. She smelled delicious. "Hello!"

Her smile was soft and sweet, her lips a pale, shimmery color nearly matching her top, and her eyes were an amazing color. Tonight mostly green, he happily noted. He stared at her for a while before she raised an eyebrow and broke the spell.

"Are we ready to go?"

Go? Go? Oh, yeah. Leave. Get in the car and drive...someplace. Harold Knox and his wife had given them tickets to the Performance Center in Tulsa for some show, hadn't they? Would it be impolite not to use them? To stay home, build a fire in his fireplace, and spend the evening getting to know one another? Yeah, downright rude, even if he could get Glory to stay with him, a bachelor minister who had to uphold what was right and proper.

"I hear we're going to see that new Broadway play," she said. "I can't wait to see it."

"How did you know?"

"Saw the commercial this morning..." Her words trailed off, as if she'd forgotten what she was saying. "Is something wrong?"

"No, no, not at all." *My mind stops functioning and thoughts all snarl—maybe I'm brain dead—when you're around.*

They stopped for dinner, but for the life of him, he couldn't remember where they stopped or what he ate. He had a vague memory of paying for the meal. And after dinner, he drove on to the Performance Center.

The wind had switched to the north and the temperature started dropping. He pulled up near the door and waited for Glory to get out.

She opened her door and hesitated for just a moment. "I don't mind going with you to park."

"There's no need." He tried to shake his head firmly, but it seemed he was unable. Instead, he smiled and gave her a long look—next best thing to a kiss. "Go on in. I'll be back in a flash."

With a shake of her head—why could she shake hers when he couldn't?—she returned his smile and stepped out. She shut the door and turned to rush into the theatre. The car was suddenly so empty, his thoughts seemed to echo off the doors. He nearly called her back so he wouldn't be alone, but that would be stupid and insensitive with the cold temperatures and stiff breeze blowing down the city streets. He waited for several cars to pass, pulled across a few lanes of traffic and into a parking lot where he was directed to an empty spot.

Glancing across the street through clear glass doors, he could see Glory waiting for him. She wasn't wearing anything particularly flashy, but from where he stood, she glowed with beauty. If he didn't hurry, someone else would certainly try to win her over. And if she came to her senses and went with someone else, it would kill him. Dead.

He stepped out of the car, locked it, and pulled his jacket up around his ears. After waiting with his hands in his pockets as a truck and two cars passed, he jogged across the street and into the building where he immediately found Glory, or maybe she found him.

Without considering the consequences, he slid his arm around her and pulled her close to his side. At least they were in a city now, where everyone didn't know everybody else. Perfect. Now he could breathe normally. Life was perfect with her there, where she belonged.

She snuggled in with her arm around his waist as naturally as his grandma's Morning Glory vines had twined around a fence post.

"It's getting colder," he murmured near her ear.

She turned her face up so she could look at him. "Yes, it is." Her voice was soft, warming him all the way through.

Looking into her face, he wanted to kiss her so badly he could barely stand it. Her lips, slightly parted as if waiting to be kissed, were nearly his undoing. He couldn't kiss her there, in the middle of all those people. Besides, she might not want it.

His heart plunged to his stomach. What if she didn't want his kiss? His attention? What if she didn't feel about him as he was beginning to feel about her? What if she was just being nice? *Then I'd better enjoy the time I have with her.* He kept her close to his side and turned toward the staircase that led to the seating.

Together they went up the stairs, taking each step in tandem.

Funny, he and Miranda had never walked that easily together. They used to laugh about how they'd been on opposite feet and bumping heads whenever they'd tried. Of course, it had been a long time. Maybe he'd learned something in the months since her death. But he doubted it.

~*~

When the play was over, Glory felt as if she'd just awakened from a long dream. The music played in her head, making her want to dance as they slowly moved with the crowd toward the exits.

The noise grew as they filed down the stairs with the others who'd just moments before been an audience. When they reached the lobby, they saw why.

The world outside had turned white. Snow and sleet was falling from the sky, and had piled up in inches.

"Oh, my." Glory muttered as they inched their way to the exit. "We'll never get home in this."

Eli chuckled softly before reaching for her hand. "Did I ever tell you I grew up in Kansas City? We learned to navigate in snow up there, or we would never get anywhere."

Unconvinced, she shook her head. "I'm not sure it's possible in *this* stuff."

They finally made it to the exit.

Glory pulled her coat close to her neck, took a firm hold on Eli hand, and they stepped out of the warm building. Her foot immediately slipped from under her. Eli caught her around the waist with one arm, tightened his grip on her hand with the other and looked into her face, a frown riding his forehead. "Are you OK? You didn't hurt yourself, did you?"

Her heart thudded hard against her ribs, making her a little light headed. "No, I'm fine. This is pure ice, isn't it?"

He nodded and then shrugged. "Maybe we should have brought our ice skates. Hang on to me; we'll make it. The car is just across the street."

They struggled crossing the street and, after what seemed like hours, made it into the car. *Might as well be sitting inside an ice cube.* But at least the wind wasn't trying to push them to Texas. Just the entire car.

"I have a feeling this storm surprised everyone." Eli adjusted the heat once he had the car started.

Shivering, Glory clenched her jaw in order to keep her teeth from chattering. "Why do you say that?"

"Because I haven't seen any sand trucks, and there was nothing but ice on the street. Usually, they're out as soon as the stuff starts falling." He switched the heat to defrost. "They must have believed the weatherman, too. This was all supposed to go north of us."

The cars were slowly beginning to leave the parking lot, but where they should have paused before entering the street, most of them slid on through. Her muscles tensed as others fishtailed and a few spun in a complete circle. How would they ever get all the way home?

Warmth slowly filtered into the frigid air inside the car, making it easier to breathe in their icy box. More cars left the parking lot, but they sat still.

"Do you have your cell phone?"

She reached for the small pocket in her purse. "Yes."

"Would you call your sister and tell her it'll be a while before we get home? Hopefully, Brandi is asleep, so she won't know how late we are."

After a nod, Glory dialed. It took a few rings, but Star finally answered.

"Where are you?" Star asked without preamble.

"Still at the PC. The roads are pure ice."

"I was hoping it was better there than here." Star lowered her voice a bit. "You should probably stop at a hotel and spend the night. The TV keeps showing bad weather yet to come."

"At least you still have electricity." *Thank you, Jesus.*

"For the time being, anyway. No telling what'll happen later, though. You really should stop if you can. Mom would die if she knew you were out in this."

"I know. At least she's not there to worry."

"Yeah. But remember your date with Jimmy North, when he tried something, and you started to walk home? It's like she has trouble radar where her kids are concerned."

Glory thought back several years to her one date with a boy from a neighboring town. How Mom had known she was in trouble, she'd never figured out. But before she'd walked a mile, Mom had been there to pick her up. "I don't want her to worry. Why isn't she gone on a cruise somewhere? Or checking on Cutter? Hopefully, wherever she is, she's asleep with her radar off. If we decide to stop, I'll call you back."

"OK. Be sensible and safe." Her voice grew lighter. "And don't give a thought to the gossips seeing you come home together in the early morning hours."

As Glory disconnected, Eli snapped on the radio and found an all-weather channel. The reports weren't good. The front the weather bureau had expected to go north of them had come farther south and stalled out right over them. They were in for a bad time, according to the newscaster.

"Why couldn't he be wrong now instead of before?" she asked, knowing there was no answer to her question.

"The heater works well in this car, and we have plenty of gas. We'll be fine as long as other cars stay out of my way." He momentarily focused on her, warming her down deep where the heater couldn't. "I grew up driving on this stuff. No problem."

When nearly every other car had left the parking lot, he shifted the car into gear. Every muscle tensing, she gripped the door handle as he drove oh so slowly onto the street.

Downtown Tulsa was almost empty, and they had yet to see a sand truck or evidence of one. Even though he crept along, easing the car down the treacherous roads, floating stop lights so he wouldn't have to come to a complete halt, she couldn't relax. Her back stayed stiff as she leaned forward in her seat. And prayed.

The frozen mix fell faster while the wind blew it nearly straight across the road in front of them, but they inched along.

Another car appeared on an adjacent road.

"Car." She kept her voice calm and low.

"I see it. We have a red light, so we'll have to

stop." He didn't use the brake, instead he took his foot off the gas and let the car roll to a stop, partly in the intersection.

When the car had passed, even though the light was still red, Eli put his foot on the gas again. The rear of the vehicle spun to the right, but he quickly released the pedal, and the fishtail stopped.

A chill ran down her spine as if an ice flake had landed on her back and dribbled its length. Letting go of the door, she wrapped both arms around herself and held on so tight, her fingertip were numb. Or was that the cold? It was bad enough trying to start out there, where the streets were relatively flat, but what about the overpasses they had yet to navigate?

"You know we're OK." Eli glanced at her, his voice taking on a comforting, gravelly sound.

"Yes." Why was her voice so tight and high? She had faith, didn't she? *Didn't she*?

He continued as if he didn't believe her. Smart guy. "Two reasons why. I told you, I've driven in this stuff since I was a kid. And two, God is with us. How can anything go wrong?"

How can anything go wrong? She smothered the scream climbing up her throat. *Maybe you're a Job, and he's allowing Satan to sift you. Or He might have a lesson to teach us. Or He might be ready to take us to Heaven. Please, God, I'm not ready for that yet. At least one time in my life, I want to be over-my-head, knock-it-out-of-the-ball-park, until-death-do-us-part, can't-breathe-without-you in love. I want to look into my own baby's face while he sleeps. And I want to see Yellowstone and the Grand Canyon.* She bit her lip until she could contain her scrambled reasoning, took a long breath and blew it out. "Right."

Releasing the steering wheel with one hand, he pried her arms loose and held her hand with his very warm one. "Want to pray about it?"

"I already am."

He flashed a half smile and released her fingers to put both hands back on the wheel.

This time when they started moving, the car went straight ahead. No spinning. When they got to the curving overpass she'd worried about, their course stayed right down the middle without a slip. Finally, they made it to the road that led to the expressway that would take them home. Except for a couple of pretty steep hills, it should be easy going. As they made the last curve before the freeway, they could see a car moving toward them too fast for the road conditions.

"He'll never make it." Eli's voice was grim as he glanced to the right.

Glory looked, too. What was he looking for? Then she realized. The road had no shoulder, and beside the little bit of area next to the road, the ground fell away to a ditch or waterway or something. But how deep was it? She couldn't remember noticing before, but then she'd never been in that part of the world on glass-slick streets before, either.

"Oh, no." Eli's voice wasn't grim anymore. It was downright tragic.

She jerked her attention back to the road in front of them.

The car that had been coming too fast was sliding

sideways, right at them. The vehicle slid backwards, then like a crazy, slow-motion ballet, it turned again. Now the driver was coming toward them, broadside.

Eli eased their SUV as far as he could to the edge of the road, but the pirouetting car kept coming. Just as it was nearly on them, Eli moved farther.

Too far.

All forward motion stopped as they slid sideways down a steep incline.

Stunned by the suddenness of their slide, Glory didn't breathe. Didn't talk. Couldn't think.

Eli thumped the steering wheel with the heel of his hand.

"Maybe we should call someone."

"Go ahead." He killed the engine, unbuckled his seatbelt and got out of the car.

The emergency operator told her Tulsa was on Operation Slick Street, which meant the police wouldn't be coming.

Eli had opened the back of the SUV and slammed it shut again. He yanked open the door behind his, stuck a box inside, and slammed it quickly, but not before she got the bite of cold air. He got back into the car and handed her a fleecy throw, which she spread over herself with a shiver.

"Good thing I didn't stop carrying these while I was in Texas." He wrapped his around his shoulders like a woman with a shawl. "They come in handy, summer or winter."

Glory gave him the news about Operation Slick Street. "Want me to call a wrecker?"

Looking through the windshield, he shook his head. "I don't think so."

"Ooo-kay." What else could they do? No way he could get that big car back up the side of the small mountain they'd just come down.

Eli started the car and shifted into gear, but their tires spun ineffectively. He waited, letting the car idle.

The heater kept her toes warm. She pulled the throw closer and snuggled deeper. Time to tell him. "Eli?"

"Mm-hmm?" He sounded so relaxed in the darkness with just the dash to light him, she wondered if he was falling asleep.

"Eli? Um." She took another breath. Why was this so hard to say? She cleared her throat and forced the words. "Brandi spoke."

He turned to her, his face so bright and his smile so big, she wished she'd told him before. He grabbed her and pulled her into his arms across the console. "Glory! That's wonderful. What did she say? When did she say it? Why didn't you tell me?"

Tangled in the blanket as she was, she couldn't get her arms around him, but she leaned into it, breathed deep of his aroma, so warm and honest.

His smile still radiant, he leaned back and looked into her face. "What did she say?"

"Nothing, really." Why hadn't Brandi said something like, I love my daddy? Something that would thrill him and make him hold her close again?

"She-she just said, 'yes'."

His brow puckered as his eyes grew stormy.

She rushed on. "And she said, 'Princess Precious'."

He closed his eyes for a moment, shaking his head. "I don't even know what that means." He turned her loose completely and leaned back against the door.

Cold air seeped through the door. Or maybe it was the look in his eyes chilling her. She pulled the throw closer. "Puppets. We were playing with puppets. She wanted to play with Princess Precious."

"When did she say that?"

The heaviness of guilt weighed into her gut. "A-a few days ago."

"*A few days*?" His voice rose in disbelief. "And you just now thought to mention it to me?"

"They were not—"

"After all the time I've spent working with her, and the money I've spent taking her to doctors, she talks to you? A babysitter? And you don't even bother to tell me."

His words stung like a slap in the face, but she couldn't blame him. He had a right to be upset. "Hey, you—"

He didn't wait to hear what she had to say. Instead, he shoved open the door, threw his blanket down in the seat as if it were a live grenade, and stalked away from the vehicle. After several very long moments, he came back and opened her door. Was he throwing her out of his car? "Come on."

He waited for her to get out, but that didn't make sense. He couldn't be that angry over three little words. So what if she hadn't told him? She'd been hoping for something better, something that would make him glad. "No—"

"I want you to drive." Anger rode his face. "I'll push."

She glanced at the slope they'd come down. "You can't push this thing up there."

"No. I can't. But I can push it over there." He pointed to a bright area, barely visible through the snow. "If there's a streetlight, there must be a street."

9

Glory glanced up from the government form she was working on to find Mom and Aunt Rosemary standing in front of her desk, staring at her. They were there to find out why she'd rolled in at 3:30 that morning. *Come on, coffee. Kick in.* "Good morning."

"What happened last night? Why didn't you get home until four o'clock this morning?" Mom folded her arms.

"Have you looked outside?"

"Of course. I know it was slick, but what could you have been doing until four? What will people think?"

Glory saved her work on the computer. She had to have more coffee if she was going to make it through this conversation. Why hadn't she made espresso? She picked up her cup and headed for the coffee maker. "That we're blessed to be alive?"

"Blessed?"

"What we got here was nothing. In Tulsa, the first of the storm was ice, and the roads were slick as glass. We got run off the expressway by a driver who was coming at us broadside. Just this side of the inter-dispersal loop."

Mom paled.

Aunt Rosemary gasped. "It's so steep there. It's a wonder you didn't roll."

"I don't know the roads in that part of Tulsa very well, and with the weather, and icy white everywhere, I lost my bearings. We wound around until we found the Twelvekiller Memorial. Once I saw that I knew my way home, but the roads were still treacherous." Words couldn't convey the sheer terror of the night. "As I said, Tulsa was hit much harder than we were."

Her mother shook her head, her mouth grim. "You should have called."

"I did. I talked to Star, but when I tried to call you my phone went straight to voicemail, so I sent you a text."

"That must have been after my battery died."

Glory sipped the steaming coffee. It burned all the way to her stomach. So good! "Maybe you should keep your battery charged."

Mom waved her hand as if shooing a mosquito. "You know they tell you to let the battery die completely before you charge it, or you'll shorten its life."

"Not anymore, Mom." Hadn't she told her this before? "Now you can charge it every night, no matter what, and you won't hurt a thing."

"Well, now that I know, I'm glad you're OK." Mom still looked pale.

Aunt Rosemary nodded as if she couldn't speak. Her face was just as pale.

They helped themselves to coffee and headed back

to their office.

Glory topped off her own drink and wandered into the daycare.

A boy was lying on his back on a large piece of brown wrapping paper with his arms and legs spread wide. With a crayon in hand, Star traced the child's outline. When she finished, the kiddo jumped up, pulled his outline over a little and grabbed crayons to draw in the nose, eyes, and mouth with the other children who were doing the same thing.

Star cut another large sheet of paper and the next child lay on it. Star called her helper take her place so she could talk to Glory. "How was it?"

Glory shook her head and smiled. "I think I'm grounded."

"I think Mom had a secret wish you'd been compromised so you'd have to get married."

Glory caught a startled breath at her words, effectively sucking coffee down her windpipe. She'd coughed, and Star had pounded her back soundly. The world was blurry with tears, but she could still see her sister's mischievous grin. "Very funny."

"I can see it now. Aunt Rosemary would hold the shotgun and Mom would say, "Exactly what are your intentions, young man?"

"Ha."

"Of course, they wouldn't load the shotgun," Star continued as if Glory hadn't spoken. "Because Mom's a pacifist at heart, and she'd be afraid Aunt Rosemary might drop it or get excited and squeeze it too tight and make it go off. If they didn't shoot Eli, they might scare him right out of here, and then where would they be?"

Glory laughed at Star's story. "Back at square one with two old maid daughters."

Their laughter drew several of the children to them.

Time to get busy. "What would you kids like to play?"

The kids shouted the names of games. Several were video games, which wouldn't work for them, but finally someone yelled, "Duck, Duck, Goose."

"Duck, Duck, Goose it is," Glory said.

When the children were finally sitting in a circle, Star was it. She went around the circle tapping each child's head saying, "Duck, duck, duck." Finally, she tapped a child and shouted, "Goose!"

The boy jumped up and ran after her, but Star beat him back to his place in the circle.

The kids usually picked Glory or Star to be the goose, so one of them was running nearly every other turn.

Then it was Brandi's turn.

"Aw, she can't do it," mouthy little Randy Boyd yelled.

"Yes, she can." Glory gave Brandi an encouraging smile. "She can do anything she wants."

Brandi went slowly around the group, tapping the heads of all the kids.

If she spoke, Glory couldn't hear her.

But when the little girl got to Glory, she whispered, "Goose!" so the entire room heard.

Glory clambered to her feet and chased after Brandi, laughing. The little girl had spoken in front of an entire room full of people. For some reason, talking was getting easier for her, even if it was just one word at a time. Glory wished Brandi would talk in front of her dad at least once.

Before Glory could tag the child, she ran right smack into a brick wall. Well, a brick wall with arms, she realized as Eli caught her to kept her from falling. "Oh. Sorry, Eli."

His eyes sparkled with unexpressed laughter. "My pleasure, Miss Glory." His soft, growling answer sent a thrill through her,

"Would you like to play with us?" Glory asked when Brandi moved to her father's side.

His eyes sparkled with unexpressed humor before he sobered. "No. I just need to talk to you if you have a few moments."

Glory focused on his face. There was something about his eyes that gave her a funny feeling in her stomach. Not quite sure what it was, she hesitated, dread stringing through her. Leaving Brandi to play with the children, she took him into her office and closed the door. Her nerves grew jangly, so she took a long, slow breath and blew it out. The excitement in his eyes as he clenched and unclenched his jaws jacked her tension yet higher.

"What?" she whispered.

His eyes widened, and he put his hands on her shoulders. "It's nothing bad, Glory. In fact, it's fantastic!"

"Tell me."

"Well, our congregation has grown so much, we have to go to two services each Sunday morning. Nine and eleven." Pulling her close, he put his arms around her. "Isn't that wonderful? We'll be a big church in a small town. Not something you hear of very often. And I wanted to make sure you and the worship team could be at both services. Worship just wouldn't be the same without you."

She didn't answer, but it didn't seem to matter. He went on talking, planning, exclaiming about how wonderful it would be to have a huge number of people crowding the pews of their church in two services instead of just one.

Even though there were already people coming through the doors on Sunday morning that Glory had barely been able to say hello to, whom she hadn't had a chance to know at all. How could a church family truly be family if one didn't recognize their faces, much less know their names?

Suddenly, he stopped talking and kissed her forehead, hard. "I love you!" Hugging her so tightly the air left her lungs with an *oof*, he kept her breathless for another moment, then released her so completely, she nearly fell.

Would he have noticed if she had?

"I'll talk to you later." He left pretty much the way he'd come—in a flurry of excitement, oblivious to anything else.

She collapsed on the old couch where her mother and aunt had sat with her between them a few days earlier. Funny, she felt as if she'd been run over by a train.

It wasn't a feeling she enjoyed. At all.

~*~

Monday morning, Glory was barely able to get out of bed. The first Sunday with the double service hadn't gone too badly, except Glory was exhausted by the end of the day. Playing for two services and teaching a Sunday School class in between was nothing to sneeze at, she thought as she dressed, and promptly sneezed. *Please don't let me be coming down with something.* She poured a cup of coffee and sneezed again.

Sitting down at her desk, she bent her neck forward to try to relieve some of the tension gathering there. No good. Throbbing started in her temples, and when she put her fingers there to massage the ache away, a tingle ran down her spine. She was warm. No, hot. Did she have a temperature? Not what she needed. Not now. She didn't even have her Bible to study if she had to go to bed. She'd left it at the church earlier. She called her sister's cell phone. "Hey, sis."

"Glory?" Mild alarm underscored Star's word. "Where are you?"

"In the office."

"Why are you calling my cell from the next room?" Worry painted her words.

"Because I feel like I'm coming down with something, and I don't—"

"Then don't come in here and share it with us!"

Star interrupted.

Glory tried not to grit her teeth while her sister finished her sentence. Gritting made her head hurt worse. "I'll run to the church and get my Bible in case I end up in bed."

"Do you know how weird you are?" Her sister asked. "Most people would take a good book to bed when they're sick or watch TV. You want to study your Bible."

"I am taking a good book. The best one. Besides, I might read some fiction, too, or watch an old movie if I can find one on TV. I just want to have my Bible with me."

"If you can wait until the kids go home, I'll run get it for you." Star's voice grew soft with concern. "Or you could call Eli or Janyce to bring it when they pick up their kids."

"I'm not so sick I can't walk over. Besides, Eli went into Tulsa to make hospital visits, and Janyce took the day off, too."

"Ooooh." Star teased. "Keeping Eli's schedule now?"

"He just mentioned it. I'll talk to you later."

Disconnecting the call, Glory stuck the phone in her pocket and left by the side door. No use making anyone else sick if she could help it. She hurried to the church and let herself in. The sanctuary was still and dark as she made her way to the pew where she sat Sunday. She tucked her well-worn Bible under her arm and hurried back the way she'd come. The throb in her head started to feel as if someone were pounding on a bass drum, and when she swallowed, her throat hurt.

She went back into the kitchen and was just about to leave when the phone rang. She picked up the receiver just as a sneeze tickled her nose. She held the phone so her sneeze couldn't be heard and then put it back to her ear. Someone was speaking as if he hadn't needed her as part of the conversation at all.

When Eli responded to the man, she understood, but before she could hang up, she heard the man offer Eli the pastor's job at one of the largest churches in California. And Eli wasn't saying no.

Shaking so hard, she could barely put the receiver back in its cradle without slamming it. The heat left the room, and she shook with the chill, her teeth chattering. She needed to get home and into bed. And maybe take an aspirin. She headed for the door. Her throat ached terribly, but she wasn't sure if it was from an oncoming illness or unshed tears.

She locked the door and walked across the grass toward her own driveway, her steps slow and careful so as not to jar her head too much. *Thank you, God, for putting me in this small town, so I don't have far to go.*

A white car with a star painted on the side pulled in to the daycare parking area. "Are you OK, Glory?" Dallas Perry asked as he got out.

"Stay there." Glory clutched her Bible and held one hand up to stop him. "Did I do something wrong?"

"No. I saw you walking from the church and when you didn't wave, and your normal smile was missing, I got worried."

"I think I've got the flu or something."

"Need help getting inside?"

"No. I'll be fine, Dal. But thanks." She started for the house.

"Sure you don't need help?"

"I'll be fine." *If I can just make it a million miles into the house.*

Glory made it to her room after a quick stop in the bathroom to take a couple of aspirin. She dropped her clothes on the chair, dragged on her big T-shirt and crawled into bed. Curling up on her side, she shivered so hard she was probably making the house shake. She just hoped the National Earthquake Society or whoever made that kind of decision, didn't take it for a real shake.

When her shivers didn't ease, she got up, dug in her bottom drawer until she found her old, ratty, most comfortable flannel gown, and a pair of warm socks. She exchanged them for her T-shirt. Digging in the cedar trunk at the foot of her bed, she pulled out the quilt her grandmother's mom had made and spread it over her comforter. Finally, she got back into bed, pulled the covers up around her neck and closed her eyes. They burned. Her ears popped when she tried to swallow, the pain in her throat hurt so much it brought tears to her eyes, which made them burn worse.

Glory needed to sleep, but her body ached so, she couldn't. Maybe if she turned on her TV, she could think about something besides feeling bad. She fumbled on her bedside table past her current book and the lamp and finally found the remote. Finding a sleeping movie—one that she liked and had seen several times—she stacked her pillows and tried to watch.

As much as Glory hated to admit it, she wanted her mother. Just thinking of her cool hands when she'd been sick in the past made Glory nearly cry. *I want my mama. I know Star called her and told her I was sick. She had to. Where is she?* She tried to remember the last thing her mother had told her. Was she going someplace to meet with her editor? Were she and Aunt Rosemary on another trip? Why wasn't she here?

Finally, Glory's eyes grew heavy, and she snuggled deeper under the covers. She dozed off just as the movie hero swung from one ship to another on a rope. Or was he swinging on vines? Not that she cared.

She couldn't have been asleep more than a couple of minutes when the door opened, and her mother bustled in with Aunt Rosemary right behind her.

Mom pushed her clothes off the chair and set a tray on it. "How are you feeling, baby?"

Her mother's soothing voice helped Glory relax. "Bad." Saying the word hurt.

"I know you do." Mom slid her cool palm over Glory's forehead. "You're hot, too. Have you taken any aspirin?"

Glory nodded, but that hurt, too.

"I'm sorry it took me so long, but I had to run to the store. We were out of star soup." Mom's remedy for all ailments was mega doses of chicken soup with star-shaped noodles in it. While Glory normally didn't like it—way too much salt for her taste—for some reason it had always made her feel better. Or maybe it was the one-on-one of her mother, which she rarely received, that helped.

"Should I go get the thermometer?" Aunt Rosemary asked from where she was disinfecting all the surfaces in the room.

"It wouldn't hurt."

Taking one final swipe, Rosemary hurried out of the room.

Mom plumped Glory's pillows and helped her sit up. "Want me to feed you?"

"No." She took a bite and immediately wished she hadn't. The pain was almost more than she could handle. Who knew noodle stars could have such sharp, scouring edges? Her throat felt as if it were bleeding. But she knew the truth. Tonsillitis had come back to haunt her again. She forced down another spoonful or two and handed her mother the bowl. "I can't eat anymore."

Mom nodded, turning her attention to the old movie. "Why do you watch these awful old movies?"

If she felt better, she'd tell her mother it was because she could sleep through parts and never miss a thing, but that was too much to explain at the moment.

"Want me to find something else? A doctor show, or one of those great talk shows?"

Even though her head was pounding, Glory firmly shook it. She didn't want to listen to people go on about their horrible lives or the people who gave them bad advice.

Rosemary finally came back with the

thermometer. "I couldn't find any of those plastic slipcovers they use to keep from spreading disease, so I brought this."

She handed Glory the device wrapped in a sandwich size plastic bag. Unable to keep from rolling her eyes, Glory turned on the thermometer and put it under her tongue, bag and all. For some reason, even that hurt. When it beeped, she took it out.

Mom snatched it from her. "Oh, my. You are sick. I'll call Doctor Pete." Mom left a glass of ginger-ale on her bedside table and, picking up the tray, hurried out of the room.

"You stay in that bed." Aunt Rosemary ordered.

Glory nodded, sliding down on her pillows as her movie transitioned to the next one. This one was about an extremely good looking angel who came to earth to help an arrogant preacher who'd left a small church for a large one and lost his faith. Silly movie. Everyone knew the preacher should be the good looking one, not God's agent.

An arrogant minister. Eli wasn't that, exactly, but she thought he had lost his faith. Was it the loss of his wife and brother that did it? Or was it having such a talent for preaching, he'd never really had to depend on God? And now, just as she was seeing his faith begin to grow, he had this new offer for one of the biggest churches in America. He was getting back exactly what he'd lost in Texas, and more.

And he'd told her he loved her.

She should have been thrilled, weak with happiness, and yearning. Instead, she felt almost, well, guilty. But why? *I do love him, Lord. I enjoy being with him more than anyone I've ever known. I love Brandi, too. So why can't I be thrilled for him to get this new mega church and do what he'd always done and probably always wanted to do?* She let her eyes drift shut and consciously relaxed each muscle from her shoulders down to her feet. Sleep crept closer, and just as she was about to drift away, a single verse came to mind.

What good is it for someone to gain the whole world, yet forfeit their soul?

~*~

"How are you feeling?"

The deep voice brought a smile to Glory's lips before she realized she wasn't dreaming. Eli was in her bedroom. Forcing open her eyes, she yanked the covers up to her nose. She had on no makeup, and last time she caught a glimpse of herself in the bathroom mirror—the only place she'd been except bed in two days—she'd looked pale as death with big circles under her eyes and her hair limp and dirty. "You shouldn't be in here."

His gentle laugh sent a thrill through her—the very thrill she hadn't felt when he'd said he loved her. "I make hospital calls every week and never catch anything. I think I'll be OK. Besides, you're on an antibiotic, and your mom said your fever is almost gone."

She closed her eyes tight and then opened them. "Be sure you wash really well when you leave here anyway."

"Yes, ma'am." His half smile warmed her. "I just wanted to see you. See if you had a response to that bombshell I dropped on you a couple of days ago."

She tried to clear her throat, but it was useless. "What bombshell?"

His smile grew as he stepped closer to the bed and found her hand. When he had it clasped tightly in his, he lifted his gaze to her face. "Glory, I told you that I love you."

At his words, the brick weighed in her gut again, making her feel almost as if she were guilty of something. But what? Why was she doing this? Why couldn't she just tell him she loved him, too? She did love him. Really. *Who am I trying to convince?*

He pulled the chair close so he could sit near her bed and still hold her hand. "You do love me, don't you, Glory?"

She couldn't help it. Holding her breath, she nodded.

"I knew you did. I can tell about those things." Pride shone in his face as if he'd just won best of show at the fair.

"What about your job?" Her throat had started hurting again. Bad. Just as it had the day she'd first gotten sick, except the pain was deeper. More intense.

He frowned as if trying to understand a foreign language. "My job?"

She nodded once as anger flitted through her and, forgetting about the covers, pushed herself higher on her pillows. "I was at the church the other evening when that man called you from California. He wants you to come out there and take over that humongous church. When were you going to tell me about that?"

"I haven't made my decision. I told him I'd get back—"

"But you didn't even tell me there was a decision to make."

"True. To be honest, I've been so worried about you; I hadn't thought much about it."

"Uh-huh."

"It's true." He reached for her hand again. When had she taken it out of his? "I understand about communication. You're so good at it, and you work in every aspect of the church, we would be perfect together, no matter where we are."

She tightened her fingers around his, hoping to squeeze the truth from him, even if he didn't know it. "But you want to take that job."

He shrugged one shoulder. "I honestly haven't decided yet."

"Why would you even consider it?" She blinked hard to keep the tears from her eyes. "You haven't been here very long at all, and our church is doing so well."

"You don't understand." Releasing her hand, he stood so he towered over her. "The mark of success for a minister is the size of his congregation. Yes, JVC3 is growing, but even if we closed down every other church for twenty miles around, we could never have the attendance the church in California has. Don't you get it?"

"Maybe you're the one who doesn't get it." For a moment, she thought her heart had stopped, but as she drew a breath, she felt its thud, slow and steady. Sounded kind of like a death knell. "Eli, I don't think God is about numbers. I think God is about lives."

"Yes, he is." He wasn't shouting, but she kind of wished he were. He walked to her door and opened it as if he were about to leave. "Every one of those numbers represents a life. And the more lives I'm leading, the better off my family is. I have to do what's best for us."

The argument sounded rehearsed, as if he'd used it before. And often. And as he talked, his eyes looked different than she'd ever seen them. He held his head at a new angle—tilted back, chin high. When he moved toward the door, even his walk looked different, as if he'd conquered the world. He shut the door quietly behind him, but it might as well have slammed.

She gathered her rasping breath, fought past the cough trying to escape and begged, "Please, wait for God to show you what—and where—that is."

But, of course, he was already gone.

Closing her weary eyes, she tried to imagine being married to the head minister of a church three times the size of Jordan Valley's population. Would she be lost in the crowd? Only see him at night, and when he remembered she was around? Or would she be able to take the huge mass of people in stride? Would God give her the gift of ministering to so many? Could she be part of such a huge gathering and still keep God first in her life?

But could she live happily without Eli in her life? If she didn't marry him and he went to California, he'd soon find a woman who'd love to be the wife of a mighty minister. Someone who'd shine like him, be talented like him and oh, be so ready for the spotlight that belonged on God.

And what about Brandi if he married someone like that? Could she love someone else's child as much as her own? Treat her as her own? Even if she had more children of her own?

Oh, Lord. Do I want to find out?

That Sunday, while Eli preached to the entire congregation, she got the feeling he was talking directly to her. She could tell by the way he glanced at her first each time after he looked down at the digital tablet. Even his topic, *Following God's Lead,* and his scripture from the Old Testament when God led the Children of Israel through the wilderness with a fiery pillar, seemed directed at her. "You can't dictate to God about His will. You have to let Him lead you."

How do you know His will? she wanted to ask. *I thought I knew that answer, but now…*

When he'd finished his sermon, he focused on her. "I'm sure you noticed Glory wasn't at the piano today." He paused while the congregation chuckled.

Should she be flattered or offended?

"Glory, would you come up here?"

Gratefulness flooded her heart as tears blurred her vision. He would ask the brothers and sisters to pray for her so that she could get over her illness. She just hoped she could climb the steps to the platform without collapsing with fatigue. Unsteadily, she pushed to her feet and, laying her Bible on the pew, she made her way to the front. Reaching down, he took her hand in his big, warm one. "Let's pray for Glory."

Without waiting to be told, many of the members moved to the front and the ones nearest to her—Mom and Aunt Rosemary judging by the fragrance—laid their hands on her shoulders while Eli prayed.

As usual, his prayer was beautiful, eloquent, and striking, reminding her of velvet covered lightning. And when he finished, she couldn't remember a word he'd said.

"Why don't you sit down here. I'll shake everyone out the door, then be right back. I'm so glad you're better."

The sincerity in his eyes made her weak in the knees, or maybe it was the heat in the room. She sank into one of the chairs on the platform and waited. She loved the old church. Loved the leaky baptistery, the creaky step up to the platform, and the podium that Mr. Miller had built by hand so long ago. She especially loved the people who *were* the church. They were more than a congregation. They were people who loved her as much as she loved them. Who stepped up and helped when she needed them. Who prayed for and with one another, wanting the best for each other without spite or jealousy.

At least they were back before they started growing like wildflowers in summer. The trouble with growing wild was there were often a lot of weeds. And it took a while to figure out which is which.

10

Eli stepped back into the sanctuary, glanced toward the front, and was struck again by Glory. Her face was like an angel's while she sat and prayed. At least he hoped she was praying and hadn't just fallen asleep—not that he could blame her, as sick as she'd been.

The stair leading to the platform squeaked, and her eyes flew open. As they focused on him, a slow, sweet smile curved her mouth.

He gazed at her, his heart warming. This beautiful woman was whom he thought of as he went to sleep at night. Whom he dreamed about and who came to mind immediately when he awoke. She filled his life. Challenged him, stimulated him, and made him think about what he would say and do, where before he'd just moved blindly forward. She loved his daughter as if she were her own. Taught her, disciplined her, and was almost as amazed by her as he was. And, miracle of miracles, Glory acted as if she cared for him, too. His heart filled until it overflowed. "I love you." Almost before the words were out of his mouth, he caught his breath, wishing he could pull them back.

Even though her brow puckered, her smile didn't

falter. Maybe she hadn't heard him. She struggled to her feet. "What?"

Going to her, he slid both arms around her and held her close. Maybe church wasn't the place to do this. It should be a warm, moonlit night with candles glowing nearby. Or at sunset on a beach somewhere. Or even in their favorite, lowlight restaurant after a fabulous meal. But God put this love in his heart for her. No matter how hard he tried to stop speaking, there was no way he could leave without making her understand.

He bent his head and kissed her and then whispered close to her ear. "I said I love you, Glory Matthews."

Putting her hands on his shoulders, she pulled back to look into his face. Her eyes filled with tears, her lips trembled, and her words sounded almost like a sigh. "Oh, Eli. I...I love you, too."

His heart sank to his knees. Not exactly a glowing response to his confession. Swallowing back his trepidation, he loosened his hold on her just a little. "Why are you afraid?" At least he sounded strong and confident to his own ears, not like the frightened little kid he truly was.

"Because, Eli, I think God made most of us to shine like stars in the sky, but he made you a blazing comet."

"Some stars are constant, never moving, never changing. Sailors can navigate entire oceans by the North Star. That makes me love you all the more."

"Never moving, never changing can seem very

boring to someone who fires up the night sky." She paused a moment, her gaze drifting away from him. "I-I'm not sure we're right for each other."

"I've prayed about this, Glory. I know that He intended you for me."

"Are you trying to gang up with God against me?" She shook her head. "Do you think maybe, we should pray about it together?"

At that moment, Brandi wrapped her arms around his legs and looked up at him with a face shining bright with love—the only person in their world he loved as much as Glory. He picked her up and held her on the arm closest to his heart, while he put the other one around Glory. Together they prayed.

~*~

Glory went home and changed into her oldest jeans—the ones Ginger hated—and a college sweatshirt, so old and faded it was difficult to read what had once been printed there. But Glory knew what it said. Comfort. And that was all she was doing today. Church was enough, as exhausted as she was. She went to her office and settled in on the couch, the most comfortable place in her world.

And then Mom walked in. Alone this time, which was unusual.

"Where's Aunt Rosemary? She didn't catch what I had, did she?"

"No." Mom searched Glory's face as if trying to read something. Finally, she asked, "Did Eli propose?"

She hadn't given Eli an answer either way. Maybe they should keep it between them until she did. But since she hadn't told anyone, how did Mom know? Glory closed her eyes and took a long breath. Eli had ganged up on her again, this time with her mother—as if God weren't enough. Mom wouldn't rest until she knew. "Yes."

Mom dropped onto the couch beside Glory and hugged her tightly.

"I haven't given him an answer."

Her words were muffled against her mother's shoulder, but Mom heard because she jerked back to look Glory square in the face.

"You haven't answered him?" Her eyes were wide with amazement. "Why not?"

"Because there's something...wrong. He's carrying a load that weighs him down, and he won't talk about it." Glory struggled up from the couch and moved to the other side of the room so she could think—away from her mother, whose opinions infiltrated even without her sharing them. "He feels that if everything he has isn't the biggest, newest, and best with the most that's the shiniest, he's a total failure. He truly doesn't understand God's leading and purpose. He's—"

"A *minister* from one of the most successful churches in Texas, and you think he doesn't understand God, but you do?" Her mother's laugh was anything but merry.

"Besides, he's been called to an even bigger church in California." Yeah, it sounded stupid. She knew that, but she couldn't help it. "I'd be lost in the crowd, except every month or so when he'd bother to look at Brandi and me. I couldn't stand that."

"Oh, California. You're just afraid you'd be homesick. But planes go from Oklahoma to California every day. You could come home anytime you wanted. Every month even, until you got used to living away."

"No, Mom, it's *not* California. It's that church. It wouldn't be right for Eli or Brandi. And if he were the minister of the biggest church in California, Eli wouldn't be right for me." Funny, how she'd just realized that. How she knew it to the depths of her soul as surely as she knew Jordan Valley would always be her home, no matter where she lived.

"Maybe you still have a touch of fever. At least, I hope that's what's wrong." Mom crossed the room to lay her cool palm on Glory's forehead. "I'm glad you were wise enough not to give him an answer. Wait until you're feeling better, and then you can." With that, she turned and left the room, firmly shutting the door behind her.

~*~

The next day, the big, brown delivery truck stopped in front of Gingerbread Giggles. The affable man who often brought boxes of books for Beany and Sam, as well as more mundane supplies, came to the door. He had two packages in his hands. One was flat with just room for a letter inside, the other was big enough for a small shipment of books.

"Hi, Clark." Glory smiled as she opened the door.

The children bounced around excited because of the delivery man who sometimes brought new toys just like Santa.

"Can I leave this with you since it's for the parsonage?" he asked with a smile for the kids.

"Sure. He's at the church, I think. I'll let him know it's here." After signing the electronic device, she took the packages from him and, with a wave, closed the door.

"What is it? What's in the presents?" Zoey asked, her voice shrill.

Glory chuckled as the other children also shouted to know. "Since my super-power isn't x-ray vision, I don't know, guys. Besides, the packages aren't for us. They're for Brandi's daddy."

Brandi stopped bouncing, her eyes wide.

"Want to go with me to call your dad?" Glory asked.

Brandi nodded.

"Me, too! I *wanna* call him!" Zoey shouted.

"It's Brandi's daddy, so she's going because she might want to talk to him, but you're not going." Glory tweaked the little girl's nose, hoping her refusal wouldn't bring tears.

"Aw, she won't talk," Zoey answered, adding her child's blatant honesty to the conversation. "She never does."

Star came into the room at that moment with the morning snack. "Who'd like graham crackers, apple slices, and fruit juice?"

The herd of kids stampeded toward Star.

Glory and Brandi slipped into the office. She dialed the church and spoke to Janyce for a moment but was quickly transferred to Eli.

"Hello?"

At the sound of his deep, beautiful voice, everything inside her stilled, warmed, and started to bloom. Why had God decided to bless this one man with so many wonderful qualities while other, ordinary men, had so few? Closing her eyes, she drew a long, slow breath. "I have something for you."

"That sounds interesting." She could hear the smile in his voice.

"It's a delivery from—" she glanced at the address label—"Laredo, Texas."

"Laredo..." He whispered the word, and as he did, she remembered Laredo was where his wife and brother had their wreck and died. "Who's it from?"

"The label doesn't have a name. It just says Hole in the Wall."

"Hole in the...what's that?"

"I don't know. Why don't you go home, and I'll meet you there with it in case it's something you don't want Little Bit to see."

"No, bring her. I don't think it could be anything she shouldn't see. Is she standing there?"

"Yes. Would you like to say hello?"

"Please."

Glory gave Brandi the phone. "Daddy wants to say hi."

The little girl nodded and put the phone to her ear.

"She has the phone, Eli." Glory spoke loudly so he

could hear.

Brandi listened for a long moment and then nodded.

"She's nodding."

After another moment, Brandi handed her back the phone and ran into the next room for her snack.

"She's gone to get her morning snack."

"I thought she probably had." Eli's chuckle sounded a little forced. "I'm leaving here as soon as I hang up. Can you come right up to the parsonage?"

"You bet we can."

She gathered up the packages and, with a prayer, went to the next room to get Brandi. "Let's go meet your dad, Brandi. You can bring your snack cup with you."

With a smile, Brandi slipped off her chair and started toward the door.

"When will you be back?" Star asked.

"We won't be long. I'm just taking these boxes to Eli." Glory glanced at Star's helpers. "Besides, you've got plenty of help. You don't need me this morning."

"No, I don't need you, but I like having you around." Star pulled a quirky grin. "Besides, I want to know what's in those presents, too."

Glory slipped on her jacket and helped Brandi into hers. Carrying the boxes on one arm, she took Brandi's hand with her other hand and left the daycare. They started up the rise to the parsonage.

Eli started down the slope to meet them. His eyes lit up as a small grin played around his mouth. "Seems like this is where I first met you."

A thrill galvanized Glory as he slid his hand down her arm, then took the packages. "Yes, but today is much nicer."

His gaze burned into hers and for a moment, she thought he would kiss her. Instead, he stooped and picked up Brandi. "How's my girl?"

Brandi smiled, her eyes bright.

He squeezed her in a tight hug. "What do you say we go sit on the porch swing and open these up?"

Brandi nodded.

The three of them strolled to his front porch.

After sitting on the old wooden swing, he set the boxes in his lap. "Which one girl, Brandi girl? The big one or the little one?"

Brandi patted the bigger box.

"That's what I thought, too." Stripping off the tape, he pulled a second box from inside the first. He pulled the lid off that box.

The most beautiful pair of cowboy boots Glory had ever seen were in the box.

"Oh, my..." Eli whispered as tears filled his eyes and spilled over onto his cheeks.

"It's your boots," Brandi said, her voice was sweet, nearly musical.

Glory's heart nearly stopped at Brandi's words, spoken as if she'd always talked to them.

Eli stared at his daughter, his mouth open in amazement.

"Eli....?"

Still gazing at Brandi, Eli said, "Open the other one, please, Glory?"

She opened the large flat envelope. "It's a letter."

"Read it." His tone was low. Intense.

She opened the white envelope and pulled out a single sheet of paper.

"Dear Mr. Daniels,

These boots were commissioned by your wife last year when she and your brother came to Laredo to order them for you. She said he was your twin and he said you were identical right down to your feet. If the boots don't fit properly, we'll be happy to make any adjustments possible.

When we'd finished creating them and shipped them to the address left with us, they were returned, and we were informed of the tragic car wreck and your loss. I just want you to know your wife and brother were extremely excited that they were able to surprise you with this gift. Please accept our condolences for your loss. We hope your little girl hasn't had any lasting injuries. She accompanied them, and I had to laugh at the time because your wife told her not to say a word until you got your boots, and the rest of the time they were in our store, your little girl didn't speak. So sweet.

Again, we apologize for the time it took to get your boots to you.

Sincerely,

Hole in the Wall Gang.

When Glory finished reading, she glanced up to see tears flooding Eli's face. Getting on his knees, he pulled Brandi to him. "Is that why you haven't been talking, sweetheart? Because Mommy told you not to?"

The little girl nodded, the look on her face heartbreaking as her eyes filled with tears, too. "I was real glad, an' even though Mommy told me not to say anything, I whispered about your boots in the car, an' then a big truck smashed into us. I made Mommy go to Heaven. I couldn't talk 'til we got them or you might go, too."

"Oh, baby." His voice was rough with tears.

Glory's eyes burned.

"You talking about the boots didn't make Mommy go to Heaven. God just happened to take Mommy when you were excited."

Brandi looked up at her dad, her eyes wide. "Really?" she whispered.

He had to clear his throat before he could answer. A single tear ran down his cheek. "Really."

~*~

Glory took Brandi back to the daycare so she wouldn't miss the afternoon fieldtrip.

Eli got his Bible and went to the mudroom—where he belonged. In his heart, he knew he was no better than a clump of wet dirt. Kneeling, he held The Word in both hands. *Thank you, Father! Miranda didn't have an affair with my brother. They fired me under a mistaken assumption.* Power rose up in him, filled his chest and gave him strength. It dispelled the unearned humility that had ridden him since his Dallas dismissal.

Now, he could prove it to the Texas church and get his position back. Or even accept that position at the church in California without concern that his past would follow him and cause problems in the future. He imagined standing in front of a congregation of thousands once more, rather than a room filled with a few hundred. The myriad smiling faces and rapt attention gave him sense of pride he hadn't felt in months.

And Glory? Of course, she'd be at his side. Playing at the keyboard while he stood at the podium....well, maybe not. While she was an adequate pianist, she wasn't exactly concert quality. The California church would probably hire professional musicians. That was what a colossal church with that number of parishioners required—concert quality. Excellence. *The best God has to offer.* Sliding one foot under him, he started to get up, his words echoing in his head and his heart. *The best God has to offer...?*

He stopped cold. What was the best God had to offer? The highest paid of all? The most studied, most learned, most excelled?

The musicians they'd had in the Texas church were polished. Shiny. Never a hair out of place. But never once had he seen a tear when a soul came to Christ. Never had they stopped playing their instrument to raise hands in worship. Never any sign of emotion or dedication to God.

No. Truth be told, they were a whole lot like he was.

Putting his knee back on the floor, he bowed his back and held his Bible close to his chest. *Father, please open my heart. Soften it and fill it completely and only with You. Help me to learn what You sent me here to teach me. Is the "best" the most talented? I don't know. Could it be that the best are the people who give directly from their hearts?*

The musicians who aren't technically perfect but who do what they do in adoration of You, Lord? Who truly worship, and don't just perform?

Father God, help me to speak only what You have for me to say and to say it in the way you'd have me to do it. Take away my studied speech, my vanity, and pride, replace it with Your words and message. And Lord, please, please forgive me for arrogance. My self-importance. Without You, Lord Jesus, I'm nothing.

Eli stumbled to his feet, surprised to find his face wet with tears. Hadn't the well already run dry? Apparently not. His heart gave a rolling thump as he thought of holding Glory in his arms. Of raising Brandi and the children he and Glory might have right here in Jordan Valley, where they would have cousins and friends and love from the entire congregation. Where a perceived mistake didn't cause instant dismissal. He couldn't leave Jordan Valley unless he knew going was God's perfect will. It was the place where he'd finally met the true God of the universe. Where he'd learned what love truly was. But what if Glory wouldn't have him? Wouldn't marry him, make him whole? He'd just have to stay and love her from afar.

~*~

Sunday morning, Glory started playing the invitation—last hymn of the morning. As she played, she looked across the congregation to see if she could tell how many people might make a decision.

Eli moved down to sit on the front pew next to

Brandi.

Heart freezing, Glory's fingers stumbled over a few notes.

Would he tell the church of his resignation? Had today been his final Sunday as their preacher, or would he give them a few weeks?

At the end of the song, she stopped playing. One of the worship singers signaled for the people to sit down.

Eli and Brandi stood.

Glory's Mom, Aunt Rosemary, and Star all move to the front to stand behind them. Eli took a deep breath and then turned toward Glory. "Glory would you come down here with us, please?"

With a nervous nod, she slid off her stool and made her way to his side.

Eli took her hand. "Glory, Brandi wants to ask you something."

Puzzled beyond endurance, it was all Glory could do to stay on her feet. She glanced at her mom and then Star, who shrugged, unable to hide a huge smile.

Brandi, dressed in a multicolored tutu and sparkly tank top—proof Eli let her dress herself— moved to where she could take Glory's other hand. She gazed up, her cupid bow's mouth grinning, and said in a high, clear voice, "Love you, Glory."

"I love you, too, Brandi." Reaching down, she hugged the little girl who smelled like shampoo and bubblegum. She straightened.

Eli was on one knee and her mom, sister, and aunt were behind him, each with a hand on his shoulder.

But she couldn't tear her gaze from Eli. His dark eyes penetrated as he reached for her hand. "Glory Anna Matthews, I love you more than I can ever tell you or show you. Will you marry me?"

"Will you be my mama?" Brandi asked. "Marry my daddy and live with us in the *pars'nage*, next to your mama and Miss Star, forever and ever, happy ever after?"

All the air in the church disappeared as Glory's throat swelled, making it nearly impossible to breathe. Brandi's face blurred and so did Eli's as Glory's eyes filled. Dropping to her knees, she blinked hard so she could see Eli's eyes. "How can you love me? I'm just...ordinary. Plain and boring. I'm small town, while you're—"

"The *Preach* at JVC3, and I'm staying here until God tells me it's time to move on. Right now, though, what He's telling me is to love you, marry you, and do my best to make you happy for the rest of our lives—if you'll let me."

He loved her. This wonderful, beautiful, talented man who could have anyone, go anywhere, be anything, loved *her* and wanted to spend his life making her happy. How could that be? Heart nearly exploding, she nodded, wrapped her arms around his neck, and kissed him. "Oh, yes. Of course, I will."

Tears streamed down his cheeks as he helped her to her feet.

Her heart nearly burst as he held her while he pulled Brandi nearer on the other side, and lifted his face to the congregation. "In case y'all didn't hear, she said yes."

And then he bowed his head low and murmured, "Thank you, Jesus."

A Devotional Moment

I keep my eyes always on the LORD. With
him at my right hand, I will not be shaken.
~ Psalm 16: 8

Standing firm in the faith is something that all
Christians struggle with at some point in their
lives. We worry we aren't doing the right thing or
saying the right words or showing God's love as
well as we should. The emotions can play havoc
with our hearts. But God understands. He gives us
ample evidence of His grace, and repeats in many
places in Scripture that our past is forgiven. While
we may still sin, a contrite examination of our
motives and plea for forgiveness is the best
medicine when we are at fault.

In **Jordan Valley Miss**, the protagonist has
everything he needs in the world, success, a wife
and child, and God. But when his life crumbles, he
questions his motives and his faith. A small town
church and its faithful members show him that
with God, life can be restored and his faith
strengthened with understanding and love.

Have you ever been haunted by things of the past,

regretting what cannot be changed? It's true that sometimes you'll have to pay some lasting consequences of some of your past actions, but once you've learned your lesson and repented of wrongdoing, don't be caught up in an endless cycle of guilt and renewed repentance. It's important to remember that once God forgives your sin, He forgets that sin. If you are continually dwelling on things of the past, you run the risk of tainting your future. Yes, if you commit the same sin over and over, you do need to amend your ways, ask for forgiveness each time you fail, and learn to trust in God more fully; but if your guilt stems from something you know God has already forgiven and some transgression that you haven't committed again, let go of the guilt. Did you know that dwelling on your past sins can also be a form of arrogance? If you're thinking about you, you're not thinking about others—or God. Remember that constantly to remind you of your past is simply the evil one trying to get you to be self-centered and to doubt God's mercy. Don't do either.

LORD, HELP ME TO STAND FIRM IN MY FAITH, TO NOT GET ARROGANT ABOUT WHAT I DO, BUT TO GIVE YOU ALL CREDIT FOR MY STRENGTH IN TIMES OF TRIAL. IN JESUS' NAME I PRAY, AMEN.

Thank you

We appreciate you reading this White Rose Publishing title. For other inspirational stories, please visit our on-line bookstore at www.pelicanbookgroup.com.

For questions or more information, contact us at customer@pelicanbookgroup.com.

White Rose Publishing
Where Faith is the Cornerstone of Love™
an imprint of Pelican Book Group
www.PelicanBookGroup.com

Connect with Us
www.facebook.com/Pelicanbookgroup
www.twitter.com/pelicanbookgrp

To receive news and specials, subscribe to our bulletin
http://pelink.us/bulletin

May God's glory shine through
this inspirational work of fiction.

AMDG

You Can Help!

At Pelican Book Group it is our mission to entertain readers with fiction that uplifts the Gospel. It is our privilege to spend time with you awhile as you read our stories.

We believe you can help us to bring Christ into the lives of people across the globe. And you don't have to open your wallet or even leave your house!

Here are 3 simple things you can do to help us bring illuminating fiction™ to people everywhere.

1) If you enjoyed this book, write a positive review. Post it at online retailers and websites where readers gather. And share your review with us at reviews@pelicanbookgroup.com (this does give us permission to reprint your review in whole or in part.)

2) If you enjoyed this book, recommend it to a friend in person, at a book club or on social media.

3) If you have suggestions on how we can improve or expand our selection, let us know. We value your opinion. Use the contact form on our web site or e-mail us at customer@pelicanbookgroup.com

God Can Help!

Are you in need? The Almighty can do great things for you. Holy is His Name! He has mercy in every generation. He can lift up the lowly and accomplish all things. Reach out today.

Do not fear: I am with you; do not be anxious: I am your God. I will strengthen you, I will help you, I will uphold you with my victorious right hand.

~Isaiah 41:10 (NAB)

We pray daily, and we especially pray for everyone connected to Pelican Book Group—that includes you! If you have a specific need, we welcome the opportunity to pray for you. Share your needs or praise reports at http://pelink.us/pray4us

Free eBook Offer

We're looking for booklovers like you to partner with us! Join our team of influencers today and periodically receive free eBooks!

For more information
Visit http://pelicanbookgroup.com/booklovers

How About Free Audiobooks?

We're looking for audiobook lovers, too! Partner with us as an audiobook lover and periodically receive free audiobooks!

For more information
Visit
http://pelicanbookgroup.com/booklovers/freeaudio.html

or e-mail
booklovers@pelicanbookgroup.com